SHRINKING VIOLET

Hi, I'm Violet. Don't go thinking I'm Lily—we may be twins but we are not identical. No way! If I'm a shrinking violet, then my sister's a tiger lily. Lily has friends and goes to parties and I—well, I don't. But I do have one thing Lily hasn't—a pen pal! I'm going to make sure I keep her, even if I have to borrow bits of Lily's life to do it . . .

SHRINKING VIOLET

Jean Ure

Ilustrated by Karen Donnelly

Galaxy

CHIVERS PRESS
BATH

First published 2002
by
Collins
This Large Print edition published by
Chivers Press
by arrangement with
HarperCollins Publishers Ltd
2002

ISBN 0 7540 7833 7

British Library Cataloguing in Publication Data

Ure, Jean, 1942–
 Shrinking Violet.—Large print ed.
 1. Twins—Juvenile fiction 2. Pen pals—Juvenile fiction
 3. Epistolary fiction 4. Children's stories
 5. Large type books
 I. Title
 823.9'14[J]

ISBN 0-7540-7833-7

Printed and bound in Great Britain by
BOOKCRAFT, Midsomer Norton, Somerset

*For my niece, Anna Ure,
and for Susanna Buxton,
who both helped.*

I am a twin. Unfortunately! It is not always easy, being a twin. People expect you to:

    look alike
    think alike
    dress alike
    talk alike.

They also expect you to:

    sit together
    walk together
    play together
    and
    LOVE EACH OTHER TO BITS.

Some twins, I suppose, might do all these things. We don't! We try our hardest not to.

My twin is called Lily. I am called Violet.

This is Lily   This is me

Spot the difference! We are *not identical.* If anyone thinks we are, it is because they have not looked properly. 'Oh! (they go) They are like two peas in a pod! How ever do you tell them apart?'

LOOK AT THE PICTURES. That is what I say.

Lily says you would have to be blind to mistake her for me. But just to make sure, we always try to wear different clothes. When we can! Like, for instance, Lily will wear black jeans and I will wear red ones. She will wear an orange top and I will wear a white one. We can't do this at school because of the uniform, but most people at school have learnt to tell us apart. They know that Lily is the **LOUD** one and I am the quiet one. It's only, sometimes, new teachers that get us in a muddle. But not for long. If one of us is shrieking, they know at once that it is Lily!

Dad calls her Lily Loudmouth because of all the noise she makes. He claps his hands to his ears and goes, 'Here comes Lily Loudmouth!' She loves to dance, and sing along to her favourite music. I do, too, but I only do it when I am at home. Lily does it all over. At home, at school, in the street, in the shopping mall . . . everywhere! I would be too embarrassed.

Dad teases me and says I am a

shrinking violet. Mum says I live too much in Lily's shadow. Lily just says I am a twonk.

Twinkle twonkle, little Vi,
How I really wonder why
Lily's brash and you are shy!

This is a rhyme that I made up, but it is in my Secret Filofax that I keep locked with a key. The key hangs round my neck on a special silver chain. I wouldn't want anyone reading the things that I keep in my Filofax! Also, I *hate* it if people call me Vi. I only did it for the rhyme. Violet is bad enough, but Vi is the pits.

The reason we've got these weird names is that Mum is a huge gardening person and her two most favourite flowers just happen to be the *dear* little shrinking violet and a great big blustering lily thing that is covered in spots and grows about eight feet tall.

How *she* got to be Lily and I got to be Violet was just a mistake. I was supposed to be Lily! I was born first (by five whole minutes) and L comes before

V in the alphabet so Lily was going to be *me*. But what with us being twins, and all babies looking the same anyway, Mum went and got us mixed up. Our nan—Big Nan— had knitted this cute little violet suit for one of us and a sweet little white one for the other, and Mum dressed us in the wrong ones! The only way that she could tell which of us was which when we were first born was by this brown birthmark thingie, in other words *spot*, that Lily has on her bottom, if you will excuse the expression. It is just as well we have now grown up to look so different because who would want to keep gazing at Lily's, pardon me, *bottom* all the time? Ugh! Yuck! What a sight!

On the day of the christening, Mum says she was in such a flap, 'I couldn't remember which of you had the spot on her bot!'

Then she laughs like she thinks it's really funny. Imagine! A mum not being able to tell her own babies apart!

But I was the one that had to suffer. I mean . . . *Violet*. It's a granny name. Well past its sell-by date. Lily, I think, is quite cool, though Lily herself disagrees.

'Lily! *Yuck*. It's like skimmed milk . . . all white and flabby.'

Dad once said that we should count our blessings. He said just think how much worse it could have been.

'Imagine if your mum's favourite flowers were nasturtium or geranium!'

Except that then I could have been Geranium, shortened to Gerry, which would be neat, and *she* could have been Nasturtium, shortened to Nasty. Which would suit her!

She's all right really, I suppose. Sometimes she can be quite nice, like when our cat Horatio went missing and I thought we'd never see him again and I cried and cried and couldn't stop. She put her arms round me and said, 'Don't cry, Violet! He'll come back.' Of course we were only little, then. It's as we've got older that she's got horrid. Mum says ten is a bad age. She says, 'When I was young you didn't start

6

throwing tantrums till you were twelve or thirteen. Now it's happening when you're *ten*.'

She said it the other day when Lily went into a simply tremendous sulk about not being allowed to go to a party wearing a skirt that didn't even cover her knickers. Mum and Lily are always having battles over stuff that Lily wants to wear and that Mum doesn't think is suitable. The reason I don't have battles isn't that I'm a goody goody, which is what Lily says, it is just that I would be too shy. Like with singing and dancing in Tesco's! She swung upside down on a handrail the other day, in full view of absolutely everyone. I just nearly died! But Lily is a natural show off. She will probably be a movie star when she is older.

Well, anyway, that is about me and Lily. Now a bit about Horatio, that is our cat. Horatio is what Mum calls 'a grand old gentleman'. He is two years older than Lily and me! Black, with a white bib.

Haratio is a *good* cat. He is a kind

7

cat. Once when I was ill in bed he came and snuggled under the duvet with me and stayed there till I was better. I thought that was so sweet of him! Dad laughs and says, 'Don't kid yourself! He just knows when he's on to a good thing.' But that isn't true! He didn't go and cuddle with Lily when she was ill. Just with me because he knows how much I love him.

So. That is Horatio. Now Mum and Dad. Dad is a computer person. I am not quite sure what he does exactly, but he goes into his office every day and does it and it seems to make him happy. Mum is a flower person. She has this flower shop called Flora Green, with a dear little green van with flowers painted on it. Really cute! Sometimes, if Dad is in a rush, she takes me and Lily to school in it. Lily

8

grumbles that it is seriously uncool, being taken to school in a van, but this is because her best friends that she hangs out with, Sarah Whittington and Francine Church, are really posh and would think a van beneath them. I don't care about such things as I don't have any posh friends and so it doesn't bother me. I like Mum's flowery van!

Lily has lots of friends. Sarah and Francine are her best ones, but there is also Ayesha and Haroula and Debbie and Jessica. Lily is tremendously popular.

On account of being silly and shrinking, I am not very good at making friends. I get nervous and blurt out the first thing that comes into my head, which is not always the best thing. Like one day when Ayesha said to me that she was going to go on a diet and lose weight.

'But I'm going to do it sensibly,' she said. 'Just a bit at a time. I don't want to lose too much all at once.'

You will never believe what I said! I said, 'No, 'cos that would look silly with a great fat face.'

I didn't mean to be rude, or to upset her. It just, like, burst out of me before I could stop it. I couldn't understand why she went off in a huff and wouldn't speak to me, not even when we were put as partners for gym. It was Lily who told me.

'You said she had a great fat face!'

'I didn't!' I said.

'You did, too,' said Lily. 'You said if she lost too much weight it would look silly with a great fat face!'

'Oh, dear,' said Mum.

I was so ashamed! I am always doing

this kind of thing. Another thing I do, I drop stuff and smash stuff. Like I dropped Haroula's genuine Victorian glass bubble with a snowstorm inside it that she'd inherited from her great grandmother. It was a family heirloom and I went and dropped it! Fortunately it didn't break, it just rolled over the floor, but a huge *groan* went up, like everyone was thinking, 'Trust her!'

Like another time when we'd been told to clear the stuff off our dinner plates into one bin and chuck plastic pots, etc., into another, and I got confused and put it all in the same bin and Lily said, 'You would, wouldn't you?'

This is the sort of person I am, and that is why I am not very good at making friends. When I do, it is mostly just one at a time; not hordes, like Lily.

I used to be best friends with a girl called Greta. We did everything together and I really missed her when she went back to America with her mum and dad. We wrote to each other for a while. I quite enjoyed writing letters, but after a bit it sort of faded out. Like I would write a really *long* letter, and Greta would just send back a postcard, and then I would write again and for weeks and weeks she wouldn't bother and then it would be just another card, or maybe an e-mail. *Hi! How R U? NY is fab! Will write soon. Luv & xxx Greta.*

In the end we stopped altogether. I suppose we didn't really have all that much in common is what it came down to. It was all right while we could do things together, but Greta wasn't really a word person. Lots of people aren't. Dad isn't. Lily isn't. Mum isn't. I am the only one in the family!

Anyway, all that was in Year 5. Now we'd moved up to Year 6 and I was sort of going round with this girl called Pandora who is very good-natured and pretty but quite honestly not the brightest. I am not being horrible here, I am just telling it like it is. She is one of those people, she is so

12

sweet and innocent she would trust just about anybody. Like she would take sweets from strangers and go jumping into cars unless there was someone to watch over her. So I was kind of watching over her because I mean someone had to and I didn't have anyone else. To be friends with, I mean.

Well, apart from this girl called Yvonne that I sometimes hung out with, but she is quite bad-tempered and also bossy, and in spite of being shrinking I don't like people bossing me and pushing me around. Plus sometimes she makes Pandora cry by saying these really mean things to her, so I only hung out with Yvonne on days when Pandora wasn't there or when I was feeling strong enough to stand up to her. We certainly didn't see each other out of school.

I didn't really see anyone out of school. Me and Greta used to meet up sometimes, but now I just did things on

13

my own. Usually on a Saturday I'd go and help Mum in Flora Green. I enjoyed watering all the plants out in the yard, and arranging the cut flowers in their buckets. I didn't even mind stacking flower pots or sweeping the floor. Lily wouldn't be seen dead in there! She would be scared her posh friends might catch sight of her. But most often she was out doing things with them, anyway. They rode their ponies in the park, or went ice skating or slept over at each other's houses. Lily has this really *full* social calendar. Her life is a whirl!

Sometimes I used to wish that my life could be like Lily's. I used to wish it *so much*. Dad always said that I was his little stay-at-home while Lily was Miss Gad About. I always pretended that I thought it was funny and that I didn't mind. I even pretended it to myself.

It is *silly*, pretending things to yourself.

One day near the start of the spring term Lily came home all excited because Sarah's mum, who is something important to do with TV, had said that Sarah could invite some of her friends to visit the set of *Riverside*.

'She said we could go next Saturday, so is that all right, Mum? It is all right, isn't it? Sarah's mum will take us there and bring us back, so can I say I'll go?'

'I don't see why not,' said Mum. 'Who else is going?'

'Just me and Sarah, and Francie and Hara. Debbie was going to, but she can't.'

'So what about Violet?' said Mum.

There was a pause. I felt my cheeks go tingly. I did wish Mum wouldn't!

'She didn't invite Violet,' said Lily. 'Just me. 'Cos I'm Sarah's friend.'

'I wouldn't want to, anyway,' I said.

Well, I wouldn't! Not with Lily and her crowd. They're all loud and shrieking, just like Lily. And they don't really like me, they think I'm freaky.

'Wouldn't want to?' said Mum. 'But you're such a fan! Even more than Lily is!'

'But she hasn't been *invited*,' said Lily. 'Not just anyone can go. You have to be *asked*.'

15

'Well, I'm sure Sarah would ask her if she knew what a fan she was. After all, she is your twin!'

Lily set her jaw in that way that she does, like it's made out of cement, or something. I felt myself shrivel. Mum does this to me, sometimes. She tries to push me in where I'm not wanted. It gets Lily so mad! And it gets me all hot and embarrassed.

'Mum, it's all right,' I said. 'I've got to help you in the shop.'

'You haven't *got* to help me in the shop,' said Mum. 'I'm very grateful when you do, but it seems a shame to miss out on other things. A visit to *Riverside*! And if Debbie can't go—'

'That isn't any reason for *her* to come.'

Mum said, 'Lily!'

'Well, it isn't,' muttered Lily. 'People don't have to invite her just 'cos they've invited me. Just 'cos we came out the same *egg* doesn't mean we have to do everything together all the time!'

'You don't do anything together any of the time,' said Mum. 'I just thought, this once—'

16

'But I don't want to go!' I snatched up Horatio and buried my face in his fur. 'Mm . . . yum yum,' I mumbled, nibbling at him with my lips.

'Stinking swizzlesticks, you're disgusting!' said Lily.

She could talk! I've seen her doing things that are far more disgusting than chumbling in Horatio's fur. I've seen her chewing her *toenails*. That is gross!

Later that day I heard Mum and Dad discussing me. They were in the kitchen and didn't know I was there. Well, I wasn't actually *there*, exactly.

I mean, I wasn't sitting in a cupboard or anything. What it was, I was outside the door, about to go in, when I heard Mum say 'too much in Lily's shadow' and I immediately froze.

I heard Mum say about Lily going off with her friends, and me not going anywhere. Then Dad said, 'She's my little shrinking violet,' and Mum said,

17

'But she *ought* to have friends!' And then a tap started running, and the sound got blotted out, and next thing I heard was Dad saying something about chat rooms.

'That way, she could meet someone with her own interests . . . that's what she needs! Someone to share her interests with.'

'Not in a chat room,' said Mum.

Dad said, 'Oh, come on! We'd monitor her.'

'*No*,' said Mum. 'No way!'

She'd read this horror story just a few days ago about a young girl being picked up (in a chat room) by this middle-aged man pretending to be a fifteen-year-old boy. Lily had said boastfully that that could never happen to *her*. She'd soon suss him out! But Mum was now convinced that all chat rooms were full of middle-aged men in mackintoshes (I don't know why she thought they were in mackintoshes), all looking for young girls and pretending to be fifteen years old. She had forbidden Lily to go anywhere near one.

She said to Dad, 'If I'm not letting Lily visit one, I'm certainly not letting Violet!'

I wondered if this meant that Mum cared more about me than she did about Lily, or whether it simply meant she thought that I was more stupid than Lily and more likely to be deceived by the men in mackintoshes.

Probably she thought that I was more stupid, although in fact it is Lily  who talks to strangers, not me. Lily talks to people everywhere she goes. In the supermarket, in buses, on trains. She just strikes up these conversations. I would be too shy! I was really relieved when Mum stood up to Dad and said *no way*. I didn't want to visit any chat rooms! It would be too much like actually meeting people; I would get tongue-tied and not know what to say.

But then Mum had an even worse idea. Worse even than Dad's!

'Maybe we could find some sort of club.'

I thought, No! Please! We'd already tried a club. An after-school club. I'd hated it! Lily had *immediately* made about twenty new friends and I'd just sat in the corner like a droopy pot plant waiting for Mum and Dad to come and pick us up.

'Maybe on her own,' said Mum, 'without Lily . . .'

It is true that I tend to get a bit crushed by Lily. She is so loud, and so bouncy! She bursts through doors like she's jet-propelled.

20

And then it is all shrieking and screeching and stinking swizzlesticks. (Her favourite expression for this term.) It is very difficult, when you are a shrinking kind of person, to have a twin that is so noisy. Everyone expects you to be the same.

Actually, it's funny, but no one ever expects Lily to be like *me*. They all expect me to be like Lily. And I can't be! I've tried. It just doesn't work. Maybe if I was on my own, people wouldn't think it so peculiar if I was a bit quiet. But I still didn't want to join any clubs!

I never got to hear what Dad thought of Mum's suggestion 'cos just as he started to say something there was this loud CRASH, followed by a series of thuds and bangs, like the house was collapsing. All it was, was Lily, coming out of her bedroom and hurtling down the stairs. She always hurtles down the stairs. Dad asked her the other day if wild elephants were after her.

'Mum!' She went shrieking past me, into the kitchen. 'I've been trying to find something to wear on Saturday and I can't! I haven't got anything! Mum, I need something new! I've got to have something new! 'Cos it's *Riverside*, Mum. There might be actors! I've got to, Mum!'

She goes on like this all the time. Like, if she's already been seen wearing something, she can't possibly be seen in it again. To be seen in it again would be *death*. It's what happens when you lead a mad social life.

Under cover of all the shrieking I slid into the kitchen and helped myself to a bowl of cereal, which is what I'd been going there for in the first place. I stood by the sink, munching it, while Mum and Lily got into one of their shouting matches about how many clothes a person of ten years old actually needs.

Lily yelled, 'Enough so your friends don't keep seeing you in the same old thing all the time!' To which Mum retorted, 'What utter rubbish!' and told Lily that she was:

    a) too obsessed with the way she looked

b) in danger of becoming shallow-minded and

c) *spoilt.*

Lily screeched that Mum was mean as could be. 'You don't understand what you're doing to me! You're ruining my life!'

This is nothing new. Dad once counted up and said that on average Lily accused Mum of ruining her life at least three times a week. Sometimes I feel like telling Lily that *she* is ruining *my* life. If she weren't so shrieky, I might not be so shrinky. Though I suppose it is not really fair to blame Lily.

At least it got Mum off the subject of clubs. By the time she and Lily had finished yelling at each other, Mum was all hot and bothered. She said she was going to go and soak in the bath and calm herself with thoughts of grass and trees and flowers.

'And not of spoilt selfish brats!'

So that was all right. But I kept thinking about it, especially when Saturday came and Lily went swaggering off (in new jeans and a new top, which were in fact *mine*). I would have loved more than anything to visit the set of *Riverside*! But you can't barge your way in where you're not wanted. Sarah was Lily's friend, not mine. I would only be a drag.

I spent most of that day helping Mum in Flora Green, but somehow it wasn't as much fun as usual. I kept thinking of Lily, on the set of *Riverside*. She might even get to see Tony! (Tony is my A1 favourite character. I once wrote him a fan letter and he sent me a signed photo, which I have on my wall.) Lily doesn't have one because she never wrote to him. She doesn't even specially like *Riverside*.

When we got home that evening, Lily was already there. She'd just been dropped off by Sarah and her mum.

'Well? So how was it?' said Mum.

Lily said that it was 'totally and utterly brilliant'.

'You know the Green, where Nick and Tina live? Where all the little houses are? They're not real! I always thought they were real. But it's just the front bits. Like you can open the gate and go up the path, but when you open the door there's nothing on the other side! It's absolutely amazing! And there's all these girls going round with clipboards and stuff. They're called PAs.' She looked at me. 'I don't expect you know what a PA is, do you?'

I shook my head.

'It's a *production assistant*,' said Lily, all self-important. 'They help the producer. Like Sarah's mum's got one called Lisa. She looks like a model! She told me all what they do. It's what I'm going to be when I grow up. I've decided . . . I'm going to be a PA!'

She strutted off round the room, holding her imaginary clipboard and an imaginary something else which she kept looking at, and frowning at, and clicking.

'This is a *stop watch*,' she said. 'I'm

timing things. It's very important to know how long a scene will take. You have to know *exactly*, down to the last second. It's for programme planning, and fitting in the commercials.'

She couldn't stop talking about it. She went on and on, all through tea. Suddenly she was like this huge fan.

'And hey, guess what?' she said, jabbing me in the ribs. 'I saw your boyfriend!'

My heart went CLUNK, right down to my shoes.

'You saw Tony?' I said.

I hated her. I hated her!

'Yes,' said Lily. 'He was acting a scene with Mara Banks, and when he came off he *smiled* at me.'

I double hated her. I *triple* hated her. I would have liked to murder her!

Instead, I raced upstairs to my room and kissed my photo of Tony and burst into tears. Why did Lily always, *always* get to have all the fun? It wasn't fair! Why couldn't I be the one who rushed around shrieking and being popular and have zillions of friends?

I once read somewhere that if you're shy it just means you're not interested in other people. You're only interested in *you*. But that wasn't true! I was interested in people. I just didn't know how to talk to them.

I could talk in my head. I could say lots of things in my head! And I could say them in letters, as well. I used to write pages and pages to Greta, when she first went to America. Maybe— sudden brilliant idea!—maybe I could find a *pen pal*?

This thought was so exciting that I immediately snatched up the latest copy of **Go Girl**, which is the magazine that I like best because it once had Tony as its centrefold. (I made a poster of him and it is on my wall with his photo.)

Hurriedly, I scrabbled through the pages till I came to the one where people advertise for pen pals. There were simply loads! I'd never bothered to look at it properly before. I'd never even thought of having a pen pal!

The first one I read, which was

no. 364, said,

✉ *Hi to all you cool cats out there! I'm Cindy. I'm ten years old and I love to party. My fave bands are Boyzone, Steps and Five. Please write to me!*

I didn't think, probably, that Cindy would find me very interesting. Not if she loved to party. I quickly moved on to the next one.

✉ *Hi, my name is Danni and I am cool! My hobbies are singing, dancing and listening to music. I am 12 years old.*

I gulped. Danni was cool! She wouldn't want to be my pen pal.

The next one said, ✉ *Hi! My name is Pippa. I'm ten years old and I just love to meet people. My nickname is Giggler!*

The next one said, ✉ *Hi, I'm Shelby. I'm 11 years old and I love parties, dancing and having a good time.*

I'm Tara, I'm Sam, I'm Linzi. I love to party, I love to dance, I love to meet people.

After a while I began to get a bit depressed, as quite honestly I couldn't see any of these cool, fun-loving people wanting to correspond with a person like me. They would soon start

28

thinking, 'Oh, this girl is not cool, she is a dead bore, I shall have to stop writing to her.' I wondered if maybe I could advertise for a pen pal myself, and if I did, what would I put?

✉ *Hi, my name is Violet. I am ten years old and I like reading, writing letters and making up stories. I am a huge fan of the soaps and my fave character is Tony, from Riverside.*

I knew what Lily would say: BIG TURN OFF.

I was just starting to despair when I came to Pen Pal no. 372:

✉ *Hi! I'm Katie. I'm ten years old and I love to draw and do puzzles. I also like to tell jokes and play with my cats, Bella and Bertie. Please write to me, I would truly love to have a pen pal.*

When I saw that my heart started beating really fast. Katie sounded just like me!

I was so excited I grabbed a pen and wrote to her straight away.

Dear Katie,

Hi, my name is Violet! I like reading,

writing letters and making up poems.
I also like drawing (though I am not
very good at it) and doing puzzles.

I have a cat called Horatio and I
love to cuddle him, especially in bed. I
used to play games with him but he
is a bit too old for that now.

I am the same age as you (but will
be eleven in April).

I am enclosing a photograph so you
can see what I look like. I would love
to have one of you, and to be your
pen pal if you would like me to.
Please write back!

Yours sincerely,
Violet Alexander.

PS PLEASE WRITE SOON!

It was the only photograph I had. Well, the only recent one. It was all our class at school, with me at one end and Lily at the other. (We always keep as far away from each other as possible when our photos are taken.) Mum had got spare copies, like for some weird reason she always does. I can't think why as they are always foul. But the only other one I had was when I was nine and looking really goofy, so I put in the school one and hoped she wouldn't notice that there was any resemblance between Lily and me.

It was only after I'd addressed the letter (to Go Girl, Pen Pals no. 372) and gone over the road to the post box that I thought what I could have done. I could have cut Lily out! I could have taken the scissors and simply *removed* her. I wished that I had! But it was too late, now. The letter had gone.

On Sunday I heard Lily on the telephone, telling Debbie all about her visit to *Riverside*.

'You know the Green, where Nick and Tina live? Where all the little houses are?'

She told her about the little houses not being real. She told her about the girls with the clipboards. She told her about Tony, acting in a scene with Mara Banks. She told her about Tony smiling at her.

'At *me*! Not the others. Just me! I know it was me 'cos the others were all looking the other way.'

Later in the day, Big Nan rang up and Lily rushed to the phone before anyone else could get there and told Big Nan about it, too.

'You know the Green, where Nick and Tina live? Where all the little houses are?'

I had to listen to it all over again. Well, I suppose I didn't *have* to, exactly, but it was kind of hard to avoid it. Lily's voice is like a really loud car horn.

On Monday, at school, she told all the rest of the class. Nina and Lucy and Jamila. Justine and Kelly and Meena. They listened, open-mouthed. Even Pandora and Yvonne hovered on the fringes, drinking it all in.

'And then, guess what?' Lily did this

little showing-off twirl. 'He *smiled* at me! Tony . . . he *smiled* at me!'

Meena squealed and clasped her hands. Lucy went '*To*nee!' Jamila fell into a pretend swoon. Kelly Stevens gave a loud screech and staggered backwards into Justine Bickerstaff. They then clutched each other and started moaning, like they were in pain. Even Pandora squeaked, '*To*nee!' and made her eyes go all big.

'Soaps are *dross*,' said Yvonne.

I was glad there was someone that wasn't impressed, though I knew it was only 'cos Yvonne was jealous. She hates it if she's not the centre of attention. (She hardly ever is, which is maybe why she is so bad-tempered all the time.)

I try very hard *not* to be jealous as it

33

is such a horrid feeling, you get all twisted up inside and it gives you a headache and makes you sick. Well, it does me. I once got so twisted up when we had a birthday party and I thought Lily was getting all the attention (which she was) that I had to go to the bathroom and put my head in the toilet and throw up. That is so disgusting! I didn't want it happening while I was at school, so I did this little hum to myself—'Ho di ha di ho!'—and went over to my desk, where I started arranging all my felt tips in order of colour. *Pink* ones, *orange* ones, *red* ones . . .

I WAS NOT GOING TO BE JEALOUS.

Yellow ones, *green* ones—

Ho di ha di ho! *Blue* ones, *mauve* ones—

'Violet?' Pandora prodded at me. 'Isn't Tony the one you like?'

I made a mumbling sound.

'*Isn't* he?'

The trouble with Pandora is that once she's started there's no way of stopping her. She's a bit like Horatio when he decides that he wants something. Usually food, in his case. He'll just keep on and on nagging at you until he gets it.

Like he'll spread himself out across your homework that you're trying to do, or walk about yowling and winding himself round your feet. Pandora just prods and pokes and keeps asking the same question over and over.

'*Isn't* he? The one that you like?'

Ho di ha di ho! Black ones, brown ones—

'*Yes.*'

Gold ones, silver ones—

'Wouldn't you have liked to meet him?'

'*Yes!*' I slammed down my desk lid. I'm not usually impatient with Pandora, but I was really trying *so* hard. I didn't want to be sick!

Lily's voice came clanging across the room.

'. . . going to be a PA when I leave school.'

'What's a PA?' said Pandora.

I said, 'Pompous airbag!' and fortunately at that moment the door

35

opened and Mrs Frost, our teacher, came in.

At first break the airbag was still telling everyone who would listen how she had been smiled at. I kept as far away as possible. I could see that even Sarah and Francine were getting a bit sick of it. The thing with Lily is, she just never knows when to stop.

Me and her went home together at the end of school. We don't always. Sometimes Mum picks us up, sometimes Dad, sometimes we get the bus and sometimes the airbag goes back with one of her friends. Today we went on the bus together and she started off all over again about Tony and how he had smiled at her—'At *me!*'—but I just took a book out of my bag and sat there pretending to read it. Not that it stopped her, but at least I was able to make like I wasn't listening. Which in fact I wasn't, as far as I could help it. I mean, bits of it kept breaking through but mainly what I was doing was wondering when I would hear from Katie and whether she would want to be my pen pal . . .

I'd posted the letter on Saturday, but I knew the postman wouldn't have come and taken it away until today. But I'd made sure to put a first-class stamp on it, so by tomorrow it would be with the magazine, and if they sent it on straight away it could be with Katie by Wednesday, and if she wrote back *immediately*—which was what I would do—then on Friday morning I could have a letter!

The post comes really late in our house. It comes after we've left, so that all of Friday I was, like, counting the hours, waiting for the moment when I could get back home and find out if my letter had arrived!

It hadn't. All there was, was a bill for Dad and a seed catalogue for Mum.

It didn't come Saturday, it didn't come Monday, it didn't come Tuesday. By Wednesday I was feeling quite despondent. I kept trying to remember what I'd written. If I'd written anything that might have put her off. I wished I'd kept a copy! Maybe I shouldn't have said about being eleven in April; maybe that had been too much like boasting. Or maybe I'd just sounded totally dim and boring.

Maybe she'd had so many thousands of replies she'd simply picked out the ones that sounded like they'd be most fun. Maybe she hated *Riverside*. Maybe I should have mentioned that my favourite band is Flying High, except that Lily says it is a nerd's band and anyway not many people have heard of it.

Maybe she'd taken one look at my photograph and thought, 'Puke! Pur*lease*!'

Maybe I was doomed to just never have a real proper friend ever, and that was all there was to it.

And then I got home on Wednesday, and there it was, waiting for me . . . my letter!

Lily said, 'Who does *she* know that writes letters?'

'None of your business,' I said.

'Who's it from?'

'Not telling!'

I turned the envelope over in my hands. It was pink and smelled of fruit and had two little furry cat stickers in one corner.

'Aren't you going to open it?' said Lily.

'Not right now,' I said.

'Why not?'

'Because I don't want to!'

'So w—'

'Lily, just leave Violet alone,' said Mum. 'Letters are personal! How would you like it if she pried into yours?'

Lily tossed her head. 'Wouldn't ever have one! Don't know anyone who still writes them!'

She can say what she likes. I enjoy having letters! I like seeing my name on the front of the envelope and I like looking at the stamps and studying the postmark and trying to guess who could have sent it. (Though I have so few that I almost always know!) I could guess that this was from Katie by the little cat stickers; and anyway, who else would be writing to me?

I waited till we'd finished tea then I rushed upstairs to my room and tore open the envelope. I'd gone all trembly because I had this fear she might be going to say, 'Thank you for writing to me but I'm afraid I have found someone else to be my pen pal.' Someone who sounded like more fun!

It is terrible to have so little confidence, but it is what happens when you are one half of a twin and the other half keeps telling you that you are a nerdy party pooper. I tell her that she is a noisy windbag, but being a noisy windbag is not necessarily such a bad thing to be. Being a party pooper is the *worst*.

I slid the letter out of the envelope r-e-a-l-l-y s-l-o-w-l-y. It was quite thick. It was three pages! I couldn't believe it!

The first thing I saw was the address, which was in London. I would rather it had been somewhere miles away, such as for instance the Outer Hebrides, as all I wanted was a pen pal. I didn't want to *meet* her! But I thought that I would read the letter first and worry about other things later.

Hi, Violet!

This is Katie, writing back to you. I was really pleased to get your letter! It came just this morning, so here I am replying IMMEDIATELY.

I would love it if we could be pen pals! You sound incredibly interesting and exactly the sort of person I have dreamt of writing to. I hope I sound like the sort of person you have dreamt of writing to!

I will tell you about myself, and then you can decide. I live with my mum, whose name is Clare. I don't have any brothers or sisters but I do have two cats. They are:

Bertie, who is small and stripy
Bella, who is small and black.

Bertie is full of fun! The other night while we were asleep he stole a toilet roll from out of the bathroom and carried it all the way downstairs,

41

then chewed it to pieces and spat out the bits. When we woke in the morning it looked like confetti! We thought someone had got married!

Bella is a sweetheart. She is very round and cuddly. She just loves her grub! Mum says she cannot decide whether she should be called Belle of the Ball or Bella the Ball!

Please tell me about your cat Horatio. I would love to see a picture of him!!

Thank you for sending me your photo. I am sending you one of me. I hope it will not put you off!!!

I noticed in yours that there was another girl at the end of the row that looked just like you! Is she your

42

sister? Are you twins? I would love to be a twin! I think it would be so neat for there to be two of you and no one knowing which was which. I said this to Mum and she said you could get up to all kinds of mischief. But she also said, maybe it would not be quite as much fun as I seem to think. Is it???

Tell me about your mum and dad. My mum is a teacher, she teaches violin and piano. She does it partly in a school (not my one!) and partly at home. When she is teaching violin the house is full of unearthly screechings and scrapings and sometimes my cat Bella sits outside the door and joins in. She thinks she is a violin!

I love to draw! I am not very musical but I think when I grow up I will be an artist of some kind. What will you be?

Underneath your photo it says 'Mrs Frost's class'. But I counted up and there are only fourteen people! We have twenty-eight in my class. I go to St Saviour's Juniors. Where do you go?

I hope you don't think I am being too nosy but it is just because I am so interested. Whatever you want to know about me, you can ask!

I had better stop now in case I am boring you. Please, please, PLEASE, write back! If you would still like to be my pen pal, that is.
Lots of luv
From
Katie Saunders XXX

PS Where does an elf go to get fit?
To an elf farm! Ha ha!

The minute I'd finished reading the letter I went hurtling back downstairs, thump thud bang! I sounded like Lily.

'Mum!' I cried. 'I've got a pen friend!'

'Really?' said Mum. 'That's wonderful! Where did you find her?'

'If it is a her,' said Dad.

'*Dad*! Of course it is,' I said. I

wouldn't want to write to a boy! 'Her name's Katie and she's the same age as me and she has two cats and her mum teaches the piano and she advertised in **Go Girl** for someone to be her pen pal!'

'So you wrote to her?' said Mum. 'That's very enterprising! Can I have a read, or is it private?'

I hesitated. 'You can read this first one,' I said. 'But after that they'll be private!'

I thought that in future letters we would probably share all kinds of secrets that I certainly wouldn't want Mum reading! But there wasn't anything secret yet, and I was just so bursting with pride. Katie found me interesting! Katie wanted us to be pen pals! I thought if Mum read her letter it would make her happy and she would stop worrying quite so much about me living in Lily's shadow.

I was right. It worked!

'She sounds lovely,' said Mum. 'I think that was such an excellent idea, Violet! Finding yourself a pen friend. I see she lives with her mum . . . I

45

wonder what happened to her dad?'

I said that I had wondered that, too. 'Maybe they're divorced?' I said. Lots of girls at school have mums and dads who are divorced.

Mum agreed that this was possible. 'But you'd better not ask her,' she warned. 'It might be something she doesn't want to talk about. Wait till she feels ready to tell you.'

'Yes, I was going to,' I said. I am not like Lily! Lily always goes rushing in with both feet. 'Where is your dad?' is probably the very *first* question she'd ask. I try to consider other people's feelings, 'cos I know how I would feel—which just makes it all the worse when I go and say stupid things like I did to Ayesha about her face.

Mum folded the letter and handed it back to me. 'It's nice she lives so near,' she said. 'When you get to know each other better, you'll be able to meet.'

I said, 'Mm!' Doing my best to sound enthusiastic.

'In fact,' said Mum, 'why don't y—'

'Look!' I waved the envelope in the air. Quickly, quickly, before Mum could get carried away and start arranging things. 'She's sent me a photo! D'you want to see it?'

I was just handing the photograph to Mum when Lily came crashing into the room. Needless to say, she had to come bundling over to take a look.

'Who's that?' she said.

I told her that it was a picture of my pen pal. 'Katie.'

'Hm!' Lily studied it, critically. 'Her nose is like a *blob*.'

'I think she looks rather cute,' said Mum. 'Like a little pixie!'

Lily said, '*Pixie*,' in tones of deepest scorn.

'Munch munch munch,' said Dad, pretending to nibble a carrot.

Lily flushed bright scarlet. Our front teeth are just the tiniest bit rabbity, so that we have to wear a brace. Lily really hates it! She is really self-conscious about it.

'Well, I'm sorry, but people who live in glass houses,' said Dad.

Angrily, Lily said, 'What's that s'pposed to mean?'

'It means,' said Mum, 'that we do not

mock the way other people look unless we want to be mocked in return. What are you doing down here, anyway? I thought you were going to have a bath?'

'Am! Don't want anything!' shouted Lily; and she slammed out of the room and went thudding back up the stairs.

'That girl!' said Mum.

I pointed out that it was all right for Mum, she was only her mother. 'I'm her *twin*!'

I decided that I would write back to Katie straight away and tell her that being a twin was not always as much fun as you might think.

Hi, Katie!

Thank you for writing to me so quickly. And for writing such a lovely long letter. I am so glad you want to be my pen pal! I am writing back at once as I know what it is like when you are waiting and waiting for something to come, and thinking that it never will and worrying to yourself in case you have said something to

48

upset the person.

First of all I will try to answer your questions! The girl at the end of the row that you thought looked like me is my sister, Lily. We are twins but NOT IDENTICAL. In fact we are just about as different as two people can be! Your mum is right, it is not always fun to be a twin, although sometimes of course it can be. Like for instance if you dress the same and pretend to people that you are each other. We used to do this quite a lot when we were little but we don't do it so often now as we are so completely different that it probably wouldn't work. And anyway Lily wouldn't want people to think that she was me and I wouldn't want them to think that I was her. No way!

What I would really, really like would be if it was just me on my own, but if Mum was to have another baby I would love a little brother! But this unfortunately is not very likely to happen as Mum says two children are quite enough for one family what with the world being over-populated and people starving, etc., and in any case they are both so busy they probably wouldn't have time for one. A baby, I mean.

You asked me to tell you about my mum and dad. My mum is called Emma and my dad is called Steve. They both work all the time, which is why they are too busy to have another baby. (Plus over-population, etc.) Dad does things with computers and Mum has a flower shop, where sometimes I help on a Saturday. Lily doesn't help. She has lots of posh friends and thinks it is beneath her to have a mum who works in a shop, even if the shop is her own one. You can see it is true that we are not at all alike.

Another thing you ask is what I will be when I grow up. I haven't yet decided! But it will not be anything to do with computers, I don't think. Maybe I could be a flower artist and make flower arrangements for weddings and parties, etc. But if I cannot do that (as I may not be artistic enough) then perhaps I will be something to do with writing. I really love to write stories! But I cannot do the pictures to go with them. You are so lucky that you can draw! I wish wish WISH that I could. All I can do is stick figures.

I expect you will say that this is utterly pathetic and the sort of stuff you would do in Reception, but it is just one of those things. I can see pictures in my head, but when I pick up my pen my hand won't do what I want it to. This is probably something that you will not understand, as I expect when you pick up a pen it does exactly what you tell it to.

It would be just SO brilliant if I could write stories and you could illustrate them! But only if you want to, of course. You might not want to. You would most probably be too busy doing drawings of your own.

51

I just loved the pictures you did of your cats! It is so nice that you are a cat person. One of my nans has a cat allergy, which means that whenever she comes to stay poor Horatio is banished. He has to go to a cattery for what Mum calls 'a little holiday'. But I am sure he hates it and thinks we have abandoned him. He probably wonders what he has done wrong when in fact he hasn't done anything. It is just my nan, wheezing and sneezing and complaining of cat hair on the furniture.

My school is called Lavendar House. It is very titchy and tiny. We have sixteen people in my class but on the day when the photograph was taken two of them were away. It is all girls. No boys! Do you have boys at your school? Most people do. Sometimes I wish that we had but on the other hand they can be a pain. A girl called Francine Church had some at her birthday party last term and they ruined everything by rushing about, shouting and showing off and spoiling all our games.

Do you have a uniform at your school? We have to wear:

Mauve blouses

Purple skirts

Brown shoes

Plum-coloured coats

and BERETS! (also plum coloured) It is so naff! Some rude boys in our road call us the Plum Puddings. Dad calls us the Lavendar Hill mob, which is the name of an old movie that he loves.

Do you like to watch TV? I don't watch a lot, except for wild life programmes (where I always make ready to shut my eyes TIGHT if there is any killing as it upsets me to see animals torn to pieces) and also the soaps, which I am a big fan of, and especially Riverside. Do you watch Riverside? If so, who is your favourite character? Mine is Tony. Last year I wrote him a letter and he wrote back and sent me a signed photograph. 'To Violet xxx Tony'. It is on my bedroom wall, right opposite my bed, where I can see it first thing when I wake up in the morning. As you will probably guess, I am in love!!!

Besotted, is what my dad calls it. He loves to tease me, and I always go bright scarlet! It is for this reason that when I watch Riverside I like it best if my dad is not there. Otherwise I spend the whole time all boiled up like a beetroot!

You know I said I don't like to see animals torn to pieces? It is one of my things and is why I am against fox hunting. I have a badge that says BAN BLOOD SPORTS. I got it off an animal stall at a summer fete and I signed a petition to the Government asking them to get it stopped.

I hope you are not a hunting person but if you are then I am sorry but I have to say what is the truth even if it makes you decide that you don't want to be my pen pal after all. I will understand if you don't only it is something I feel quite strongly about. I just felt that I had to say it. I hope you will not be offended as I don't mean to be rude or anything.

I must go now as Lily has just got out of the bath and Mum is yelling at me that it is my turn. What time do you have to go to bed? I have to go at nine thirty in the week and half-past ten on Fridays and Saturdays. It is too early, if you ask me, but Mum says I will thank her for it when I am older. She says if you don't get enough sleep you start to LOOK YOUR AGE. I don't know about you but I would quite like to look my age. One of Mum's friends the other day asked me when my birthday was. She said, 'And how old will you be? Ten?' It is so insulting!

I do hope you will write back to me and not be angry at what I said about fox hunting. But please don't feel you have to do it immediately! (Though it would be lovely if you did.) I am sure you are very busy, especially if you have lots of homework. We have OCEANS. I don't really mind, except if it takes too long when I would rather be writing to you!

Love from your pen pal,
Violet
xxxxxxxx

PS   Someone told me this joke at school the other day.

Question: What is green and slithers and goes 'hith'?
Answer: A thnake with a lithp!

PPS Here is a photo of my cat Horatio: You can keep it if you like.

I posted the letter on my way to school next day. The very minute that it plopped into the box I started to worry! Dad says I am a regular worry guts and I know that he is right. I don't only make mountains out of molehills, I make them out of microdots! I just can't seem to help it.

These are some of the things I worried about:

1.   Fox hunting. Why did I have to go and mention it??? It is true that it is

something I feel strongly about, but it is not the only thing. I feel strongly about lots of things! For instance: people starving, and babies dying of AIDS, and global warming, and land mines. To name just a few. I didn't go and mention them! Now I had probably upset her and wouldn't ever hear from her again.

2.   The second thing was saying I'd gone to Francine's party when I hadn't. Not that I'd actually *said* that I'd gone, just made it read like I had. Telling her about the boys and how they'd ruined things, rushing around shouting and spoiling all our games. I was just repeating what Lily had said. She was the one that had gone to the party, not me! Why had I done it???

3. The third thing was saying how we had to wear those hideous berets and how our school uniform was naff. But I like our school uniform! Lily's the one that thinks it's naff.

I suppose I was trying to be cool. Which is truly pathetic! But going on about fox hunting, that was really *dumb*. There's a girl at school, Justine Bickerstaff, that in the hunting season she gets on her horse and gallops madly about the countryside with packs of hounds. She has even done this *revolting* thing called cubbing, where they tear dear little sweet innocent fox cubs to pieces. I hate that! I hate that so much. But Justine gets into this simply mega-rage if anyone ever says about banning blood sports. For all I knew, Katie could be the same. And I had gone and lectured her and now I had probably RUINED EVERYTHING.

I was just so relieved when I got her next letter. All that worrying, all for nothing! (It usually is, but I still do it.) I knew as soon as Mum handed me the envelope that things were all right.

Instead of the little furry cat stickers there was one that said, STOP HUNTING WITH HOUNDS. So I hadn't upset or offended her! She was on my side. Hooray!

'Is that from the Blob?' said Lily. 'Are you going to open it this time?'

I said, 'No. I like to read my letters in private.'

Lily tossed her head and said, 'Letters! You're so uncool. Why don't you e-mail?'

'You could, you know,' said Dad.

He's always trying to get me on the computer. I am not terribly awfully into them, to be honest. Lily is. She is on it the whole time, whizzing about doing things, sending e-mails to all her friends. She sees them all day and e-mails them all night! When she is not text-messaging on her moby.

'Think about it,' said Dad. 'It would be far more fun than scribbling on bits of paper!'

'But *she* might read them,' I said.

'Me?' Lily gave a hoot of laughter. 'Who'd want to read what you and the Blob have to say to each other?'

Dad said, 'Violet, I give you my word, nobody but nobody would read your e-mails. They would be for your eyes only.'

That's what he *says*. But I bet she'd still find a way!

'Why not ask?' said Dad. 'Ask her if she'd like to.'

I said that I would, 'cos I like to make him happy and it is true that most people seem to prefer sending e-mails to writing real letters. Maybe if I'd e-mailed Greta we would still be in touch.

As soon as tea was over, I rushed upstairs to my room. (Mum calls it my *burrow*.) I tore open the envelope and a whole wodge of paper fell out. Which is far more fun than e-mails, if you ask me!

Hi, Violet!

Don't worry, you have not offended me! I HATE people that kill foxes. So does my mum. We have both filled in petitions against it. If I see a badge I will buy one and wear it.

I laughed over your snake joke! Here is one for you. A joke, I mean. Not a snake joke. (It is a knock-knock joke.)

Knock knock!
Who's there?
Ivor.
Ivor who?
Ivor let me in or I'll break the door down!

Har har!

Your school uniform doesn't sound naff, it sounds fabbo! I love berets! Ours is just green. Green everything! It makes us look like gooseberries. And yes, we do have boys. Yeeurgh! You are so lucky, not having them. They are such a nuisance. Well, I think they are.

What will happen when you change schools? Where will you go? I will probably go to Friars Stile, which is just down the road. Mum doesn't really want me to, she says it is too big and too rough, but all my friends would be going there. Will you be able to stay with your friends? Do you have lots of them? Do you like to party?

I laughed when you said about boys rushing round shouting! This is what they do ALL THE TIME. Susanna, one of my friends at school, is having her birthday party next week but she is not going to invite any. Boys, I mean! She is just inviting girls from our class. It will be such fun! I would go to parties non-stop if I could. I will tell you all about it in my next letter!

You asked if I like to watch TV. The answer is . . . yes! But I like to draw and paint and read books as well. Riverside is my ace fave soap, and I think Tony is gorge! Even Mum says he is a hunk. I am so envious of you, having him on your wall! Do you kiss him goodnight before you go to bed? I would!

I am sorry it is not fun to be a twin. Mum said, 'I told you so!' She also said what nice names you have. Lily and Violet. She says, 'I hope they are not shortened to Lil or Vi, as this would be a shame.' Are they???

I am a bit like you, I would love it if Mum would have another baby but I don't think she will as the only man friend she has is rather old and I cannot see that they would ever get married. He is called Arthur and has grey hair but is very nice. He is like a granddad. Mum enjoys going to the theatre with him, and sometimes we all visit places in his car.

You know you said that you and your sister are not identical? I have looked VERY HARD under a magnifying glass, and I don't see how anyone could tell you apart! I hope you are not cross with me for saying this. I can quite understand that you are two different people, for instance your sister will not help your mum in her shop because of her posh friends. Whereas you do not mind about such things. Do the posh friends go to your school? Is it a posh sort of school?

I hope you don't think I am prying or being nosy. Like I said before, you can ask me ANYTHING. I will not mind!

Bertie has just been chasing his cat nip toy. He is so sweet! He jumps in the air and claps his paws.

I am glad you like my drawings, and I do understand what you say about your hand not doing what you want it to. It is the same with me and singing. I can hear all the notes as clear as can be in my head but then when I open my mouth they just come out all wrong. Mum says I sound like a lovesick hen! She has to put her hands over her ears.

Here is a game. Close your eyes and do a scribble on a piece

of paper, then send it to me and I will make a picture of it.
Like this:

This is GENUINE. I closed my eyes and did the scribble, then I traced it (so you could see what it looked like) and then I made the picture. I play this game all the time, but it would be ever so much more fun to play it with someone else. It doesn't matter if you can't draw! Anyone can play the scribble game.
I'll do one for you, if you like.
You don't have to make a picture

if you don't want to! But if you do then I'll make one as well and we can compare them. It will be interesting to see what different things we make! But only if you want to. I'm going to trace the scribble right now.

I've traced it. Now I'm going to put this letter in an envelope and tomorrow on her way to work Mum will post it. Write soon!
Luv and kisses
From
Katie

PS   I have drawn a maze for you! See if you can find your way in.

PPS Thank you for your photo of Horatio. He is very handsome! I am going to put him in a frame next to my ones of Bella and Bertie.

After I'd read Katie's letter I was glad that I'd told her about Francine's party. Even if I hadn't been there! I mean, I hadn't actually told a lie. Not straight out. But Katie was starting to sound a whole lot more cool than I'd thought she was going to be. Nobody who thought it would be fun to party non-stop would want to go on writing to a nerdy stay-at-home, which is what Lily calls me. (When she's not calling me a twonk, or a party pooper.) I really wanted Katie to go on writing! I loved the jokes that she told and the little drawings that she did and the way she played with her cats and the games that she invented. Surely it wouldn't matter if I just pretended once or twice? It wasn't like we were going to be meeting-up-and-getting-together sort of friends. Just pen pals!

I spent ages trying to turn her scribble into a picture. I think perhaps I cheated as I made lots of copies on Dad's photocopier so's I could have lots of goes. I didn't want her to think I was *completely* useless. Although I am! Lily can draw quite well. It is so unfair because she doesn't even enjoy it, particularly. She would rather do graphics on the computer. On the other hand she is not much good at writing. She can't spell for toffee and her essays are only ever about one page long, and that is using REALLY BIG

TYPE. Mine are sometimes five pages, or even six! Mrs Frost writes little notes at the end like 'Very inventive use of language!' or 'You have a good imagination, Violet.' She has never said that about Lily!

But Lily could have done cleverer things with Katie's scribble. If she could be bothered, which most likely she wouldn't. This is the best that I could do:

A sort of . . . *thing*. But I did the maze all right!

I showed Katie's drawing of Bertie playing with his cat nip toy to Mum. I didn't show her the letter because by now things had started to become a bit private, but I wanted her to see Bertie.

'He's so cute,' I said, 'isn't he?'

'Like a little stripy tiger,' said Mum. 'She's very good at drawing, isn't she?'

'Yes, and she just loves Bella and Bertie,' I said. 'She plays with them all the time. Specially Bertie. He's really mischievous!'

'Like Horatio used to be,' said Mum.

I said that I couldn't remember Horatio ever playing, but Mum said that was because he was two years old when I was born.

'Cats don't stay kittenish very long.'

'I suppose,' I said, trying to sound casual, 'we couldn't have one, could we?'

'One what?' said Mum.

I said, 'A kitten!'

Mum laughed. 'Is that what all this has been leading up to?'

'Mum! No!' I said. I put on this very

hurt and surprised expression. 'I just suddenly thought it would be fun.'

'Just suddenly?' said Mum.

'Well . . . fairly suddenly.' Like immediately after reading Katie's letter! 'Mum, please!' I said. 'Couldn't we?'

Sometimes, if I really beg and plead, I can get round Mum. Lily says I am a right creep. She says I play at being little shrinky winky Violet and Mummy's girly. Lily would rather rant and roar and yell that Mum is ruining her life. Sometimes Mum gives in, just for the sake of peace and quiet, like sometimes she gives in to me because I have asked *nicely.* Sometimes! Not always. This was one of those times when she didn't.

She said that Horatio was too old to cope with a kitten. It wouldn't be fair on him.

'Why don't you ask Katie if you can go over and play with hers?'

'Mum, we're *pen* pals,' I said.

'So? That's no reason you shouldn't get to meet each other!'

I said, 'But then we wouldn't be pen

71

pals.'

'Of course you would!' said Mum. 'There's nothing to stop you being both.'

I didn't want to be both! I just wanted to be pen pals. I almost began to wish that I'd never told Mum about Katie. I only did it 'cos I thought it would please her. Now she was going to start nagging at me to do something I didn't want to do. She was going to ruin everything!

'All right, all right,' said Mum. 'Calm down! No one's going to force you.'

'I just want to write letters,' I said.

Mum said in that case, writing letters was all I need do.

'Whatever makes you happy.'

And then she hugged me and said, 'Cheer up! No one's having a go at you!'

I wondered to myself whether Katie's mum nagged her to do things. I thought probably not. Katie wasn't shy! She went to parties and had lots of friends. I wished I could think of something interesting and exciting to tell her, to stop her getting bored with me. But I don't ever do anything interesting or exciting! Not what other people would think was interesting or exciting. It was Lily that did things. Like going to visit the set of *Riverside*. That was interesting. And exciting! And I'd heard all about it in the hugest detail . . .

Dear Katie,

Hi! I have something very exciting to report. I went with my friend Sarah and her mum to visit the set of Riverside!!! It was just fantastic!
 You will never guess what happened! Tony was there and he smiled at me!!! I thought I would just die! He is every bit as gorgeous in real life as he is on the screen. Sarah was SO jealous, 'cos she likes him, too. It was a moment I shall treasure for always.
 How was your party that you were going to? The one without boys? I am dying to hear about it! I want to know everything you did.
 Now I am reading through your

letter to see what questions you ask. By the way I don't think you're prying or being nosy! I think it is only natural to want to know each other.

Please tell your mum that Lily and me get mega-mad if anyone dares to shorten us to Lil or Vi! We think that Lily and Violet are quite bad enough. It is because of them being my mum's favourite flowers. I mean, that is why we are called them. But we think they are HIDEOUS!

I am really surprised that you like our school uniform! Personally I would rather be a gooseberry than a plum pudding, but I am stuck with being a pudding until Year 12, when I will probably go to sixth form college as there is no sixth form at our school. I told you it is very titchy and tiny. (Though you can stay there until you are sixteen.) I don't think it is posh, exactly, even though there are some posh people that go there. But most of us are just ordinary. At the moment I think it is nice that there are no boys, however Mum says this may change as I get older. I don't think so!!!

And now ... ssh! I do kiss Tony every night. But don't tell anyone! Not even Lily knows. She would laugh at me if she did.

I am not cross with you for saying that we look the same. Lots of people think this. Usually it is because they do not look properly. I know you said that you looked with a magnifying glass, but the photograph I sent you was taken last term. We have changed A LOT since then. And when two people are very different I think it has to show in their faces even if they did come from the same egg.

I hope it does not embarrass you, me saying about eggs. It is only biology. But I once said it to this girl Pandora that is in my class and she turned very red and said that I was rude to talk about such things. But she is a very odd sort of girl.

You are not the only one who

cannot sing. Nor can I! I cannot sing and I cannot draw. I think it is so annoying when you cannot do things that you would like to be able to do. When I sing my dad says I sound like a toad with tonsillitis. Could you draw a picture of that? Then I would be able to show it to my dad and he would laugh.

I want to ask you something. Do you let your mum read your letters? I don't let anyone read mine, except just your first one I let my mum see. But not now! Now they are STRICTLY PRIVATE, even though Lily would just love to get her hands on them. But I won't let her. Don't worry!

Oh, I have just remembered. Dad says, why don't we e-mail, instead of writing letters? He says it would be more fun. Do you think that it would? If you would like to e-mail, then we can do it. I don't mind.

I made a picture out of the scribble, but I'm afraid it is not very good.

Thank you very much for the

maze, which I managed to find my way into. I don't mean to boast, but it was quite easy. Can you do another one and make it more difficult?

I have a game for you! Guess what musical instruments these are:

Teful
Tigura
Novili
Glube

I have just made this up!

Do you like playing word games? I can think of loads more! Sometimes what I do, like when I am travelling on the bus for example, I look at the advertisements and I find a word and I see how many other words I can make from it. Like yesterday me and Lily had to go to school by ourselves because of Mum and Dad being too busy and there was this huge traffic jam and Lily got all twitchy and impatient but I just sat there making up words.

The word I made them from was INSURE. Sitting on the bus I only made up nine, but that was in my head. I have just done it again and this time I have made up twelve! If you like, I will tell you what they are. I will do it at the end of this letter. It is just a game, but it is quite fun.

Next week my class is going to visit the British Museum. After we have been there we are going to write stories about mummies. Egyptian ones, I mean! I am really looking forward to it!

Please write back soon and do another maze. I hope I have not upset you by saying the one you sent was easy. It wasn't as easy as all that! I think you are very clever, being able to draw mazes.

That has made me think of a joke: I am totally a-MAZED.

Ho ho! Must go!

Lots of luv

Violet xxx

PS TOP SECRET!
These are the words I made but DO NOT READ THEM until you have seen how many you can make! By order!!!

Ire rue rise run ruin rein rinse sure sin sun sue nurse

I expect you may be able to find more.

PPS I think it is cool to have a 'granddad' called Arthur. I have only one granddad. He is called James. He is my mum's dad. Going now.

Byeee!

I put in the bit about granddads in the hope that maybe next time Katie would tell me about her dad. I still didn't like to ask. I know she said 'Ask me anything. I don't mind,' but I remembered when Kelly Stevens' mum and dad split up. Kelly was in tears for weeks. I didn't like the thought of Katie being in tears. Her photo made her look so bright and perky! She looked like a really happy sort of person.

On Tuesday we went to the British Museum. The whole class, with Mrs Frost and another teacher, Miss Adams, to keep us in order. Some of us need keeping in order! Lily and her friends just behave *so* badly. Even on the tube they couldn't keep quiet but shriek and giggle and swing to and fro on the handrails. Lily kicked someone and had to apologise, and Sarah almost fell into the lap of a man that was reading his newspaper. She went, 'Oops! Sorry!' and giggled. She didn't seem at all embarrassed. I would have been! I would just have died.

Miss Adams told them to calm down. She said, 'Lily! Sarah! Please!' But nobody ever takes any notice of Miss Adams. She is one of those teachers, she just has no idea how to control us. Not like Mrs Frost. She can be quite fierce! But Mrs Frost was way down the far end and couldn't see what was going on. By the time we got out at Tottenham Court Road, Lily and Sarah were giggling and shrieking at just about everything.

'Ooh! Look. Panties!' shrieked Sarah, as we went up the escalator, past all the adverts. Lily screeched.

'*Panties*!' she went.

I don't know what they found so funny about it. I mean, everyone has to wear them, even the Queen. (Unless they're a nudist, which I personally wouldn't want to be as I would almost certainly break out into goose pimples.)

'Pantyhose!'

'Chest hair!'

'Ooh, look, there's a naughty one!'

They giggled and shrieked all the way up the escalator. By the time we reached the museum they were totally hyper. Mrs Frost spoke to them, quite sternly. She said that unless they pulled themselves together and stopped acting like five year olds she would send them straight back to school with Miss Adams.

So then they went a bit quiet and crept round on exaggerated tiptoe, silently pointing at things and pulling faces. Every now and again Mrs Frost would check them out. She'd shoot them one of her dagger glances and they would stare soulfully back with these hurt expressions on their faces. Lily can look just *so* angelic when she wants to.

I walked round with Pandora. I would rather not have walked with her as I was trying to make mental notes of everything I saw so that I could report back to Katie next time I wrote. It is very difficult to make mental notes when someone is constantly wittering at you, but Pandora is a person that just kind of *sticks*. Unless you are rude there is no getting rid of her. I didn't want to be rude as she is very easily hurt, she crumples at the least little thing, so I did my best to shut out her wittering and hoped that I would remember a few interesting things to tell Katie. She was going to tell me about her party, so I had to have something to tell her in return!

It was the mummies we all wanted to see. They were quite spooky! I'd seen m u m m i e s before, of course, on television and in books. But never in the f-f-f-flesh!

Not that mummies have flesh, really. Not that you can see. They are all done up in bandages. You can only imagine what lurks beneath . . .

Fortunately they are all kept in glass cases, otherwise I would probably have had visions of them getting out and walking round the museum at dead of night, like in a film I once saw. I was only quite little and I had to keep hiding my head in a cushion. Mum said afterwards that I shouldn't have watched it. I do have this rather over-active imagination.

Lily doesn't have any imagination *at all.* To her a mummy is just a dead guy. This is what she yelled—'Dead guys!'— as she went shrieking off with Sarah across the polished floor. Pandora clutched at my sleeve and said, 'Are they really dead?'

'Well, they're not *alive*,' I said.

'But are they real people?'

I told her that they had been, once; a long time ago.

'So if you took the bandages off . . . what would they be like?'

'Just sort of . . . *skin*,' I said. 'All dried and withered. 'Cos there's nothing inside them. It's all been taken out. All their organs,' I said. 'Their intestines, and their livers, and their lungs . . . they used to take them out and put them in special jars.'

Pandora's lip quivered. 'While they were still alive?'

I said, 'No! When they were dead.'

We'd already done all this at school, but Pandora's a bit slow at taking things in. She always has to be told several times over. It is no use being impatient with her. Something happened when she was born and made her not quite right. Maybe for all I know something happened when I was born and made me not quite right. Maybe that is why I am a shrinking violet and it is not my fault any more than it is Pandora's fault that she keeps asking stupid questions all the time.

While we were talking, Lily and Sarah had been racing excitedly from mummy to mummy. All of a sudden, Sarah shrieked, 'Hey, look at this one! Who does he remind you of?' Naturally we all went running over to look.

'It's Mr Spooner!' cried Lily. 'What is he doing here?'

We all collapsed! We just couldn't help it. Poor Mr Spooner! He is one of our teachers at school.

'Mr Spooner,' said Pandora, gazing at the mummy.

Just then, Mrs Frost came over to

85

see what we were giggling at. She must have heard what Pandora said! I could see her lips start to twitch, as if she would have liked to giggle, too. I mean, that mummy really did look like Mr Spooner! But of course, being a teacher, she couldn't let herself.

We all stopped giggling except for Pandora, who had only just started. The rest of us made like we were sucking on lemons. Disgraceful! Quite disgraceful!

Mrs Frost shook her head. 'Without any doubt,' she says, 'you are far and away the worst bunch I have ever had to deal with!'

After that we all went for snacks in the cafeteria then back to the station to catch the train home. And I've gone and forgotten every single mental note

that I made! All I can think of to tell Katie is Mrs Frost saying we're the worst bunch she's ever had to deal with . . .

Good morning! This is me. Katie!

How are you? I think your scribble picture was really good! Some people that in the past I have tried to play it with, they have just had no imagination at all. It is no fun when people have no imagination.
The maze that I sent you was one I did in a hurry as I wanted you to have it. I have done another one that is more difficult. I like drawing mazes. It is something I have only just started doing. I didn't mind you saying the first one was too easy, though a maze doesn't always have to be difficult. There are some that are just pretty. My one wasn't but that was because I didn't have time.
I loved hearing about your visit to Riverside. I am just SOOOO

envious! If I was smiled at by Tony I think I would swoooooooon. I would never recover! I knew about the little houses not being real because I read about it somewhere but I would still very much like to go and see them. If I didn't swooooon!

I told Mum about you not liking to be called Lil or Vi. She says she is glad. But we don't know why you don't like your names! Mum says they are charming and unusual. I think Violet is nice as I just happen to love violets. They are so sweet and dainty! I don't like Lily so much. (But don't tell her I said so!!!) I think lilies are a bit too pale and droopy. They smell nice, of course. But so do violets! Plus you can have violet chocolates. I never heard of lily chocolates!

Here is you and your sister:

It didn't embarrass me, you saying how you both came out of the same egg. We have already done this at school, so it is

something I know about. How silly
of that girl Pandora to go red! As
you say, it is only biology. She
must be really weird. There is a
girl in my class that is weird. She
is called Shayna and she eats
flowers! Our teacher once told us
that you could eat nasturshums
(?) and so now she eats every
flower she comes across. Nothing
is safe from her! Last week there
was a bowl of hyercinths (?) in the
hall and she picked off the top
and devoured it! Mrs Glover (our
teacher) says that she will make
herself ill, but still she goes on
doing it. Mum thinks that maybe

she is feeling neglected and it is her way of drawing attention to herself. I think she is just loopy.

I have drawn a picture for your dad of you being a toad. I will cut it out and stick it on NOW.

I agree it is sad when you cannot do things that you would like to do. It is very frustrating. Especially when there are people that can do them that don't particularly want to. Then you think to yourself that they do not know how lucky they are and that life is so unfair. Only I try not to think that too often as it is what Mum calls COUNTER PRODUCTIVE. Meaning: it doesn't get you anywhere! It just makes you bitter and unsatisfied.

No, I don't show Mum your letters!!! No way!!! I tell her things that I think will interest her and that I think you will not mind if I tell her, like for instance about you

being a twin. That sort of thing.
But nothing private!

I do like to play word games,
even though I am better at the
drawing ones. I worked out all the
musical instruments! I will draw
them for you.

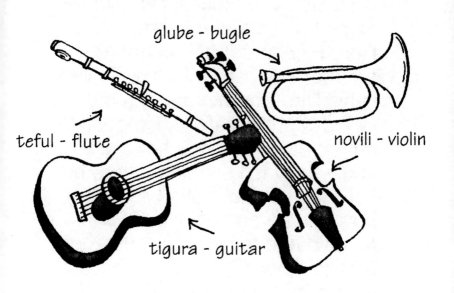

glube - bugle

teful - flute

novili - violin

tigura - guitar

But I could only make seven
words out of that word you gave
me. The ones I didn't get were:
ire, rue, rein, sue, rinse. I asked
Mum if she could do it and she
got the same as you! She says

you must be very good at English. I am afraid you will think I am rather ignorant as I had never heard of the word ire! Please don't be shocked. I have heard of it now and I will remember it.

Mum told me what it meant. She said it is another word for RAGE, which is what I felt last week at school when a stupid boy called Rory McArthur bashed out at another boy (Kevin Halliwell, who is his Dire Enemy) and got my friend Yasmin instead. He got her on the ear and made her cry. I know he wasn't aiming at her, but I still felt ire. He is such a clumsy boy, and so aggressive. Poor Yasmin had to go to the rest room and lie down. Rory got a good telling off. But he will just go and do it over again. There is nothing that can stop him. He and Kevin have this hate thing, and anyone that gets in the way, well that is just too bad. BOYS. puke!

We are on half-term! Are you? If so, are you doing anything

exciting? I am just staying home with Mum but we are playing lots of games and having fun.

Oh, you asked me about e-mails! I am afraid we do not have a computer. I am really sorry about this, Mum says we will have to get one some time but not just yet as she has too many bills to pay. I expect Arthur would get one for us if Mum told him I wanted one, but Mum always says she is not going to SPONGE. In other words, we must make do and be independent. I know she is right and I am not complaining. But meanwhile we will have to be pen pals by snail mail, if this is all right with you?

I hope you will not mind. There are a lot of things that other people have that we do not. For instance, a video. For instance, a microwave. For instance, a dishwasher. A girl at school called Carrie Francis once asked me how we survive. She says it must be like living in the 1940s house that they showed last year on TV. Did you watch it? I was like GLUED to the set, it was so fascinating. Seeing how people lived! But Carrie is just stupid to say that me and Mum live like that. We don't! We have central heating and a television and a washing machine, just like everyone else. We are not primitive! That girl really gets on my nerves at times.

Now for the exciting bit! I have been keeping it till last. THE PARTY!

It was the hugest fun! It was held in a hall, and there was this DJ called Ryan who organised everything and did Prince Charles impressions. He looked just like him! It was really funny.

There were thirty of us in all. NO BOYS. Carrie Francis arrived wearing a tall white floppy hat with a smile on it. She kept batting her eyelashes at the DJ, trying to make him fancy her. (Which he clearly didn't!) Suaanna, the one that was having the party, said she was way over the top. In the end Susanna's mum had to step in and tell her to calm down.

You will want to know what we did. Well, we danced a lot! The bands we danced to were S Club 7 and Steps. (Two of my favourites!) He also played 'Sex Bomb' by Tom Jones, which Susanna's dad didn't approve of! Susanna says he is not very cool. But anyway there was nothing he could do to stop it!

As well as dancing there were also lots of songs that you do the actions to, such as 'Superman' and 'Macarena' by Los Delrio. We also had a limbo contest using the DJ's microphone stand, plus a game where there were three teams and we had to pass a balloon over, then under, from person to person. Phew! I think that DJ wanted to tire us out. Which if he did he certainly managed it, as by the end even

Carrie Francis had stopped batting her eyelashes. Oh, and her tall floppy hat wasn't tall any more! She took it off and put it on a chair while we were doing the limbo and a girl called Abbie that is rather BIG, went and sat on it and squashed it flat. So now it was a squashed floppy hat! It looked ridiculous. Well, it looked ridiculous to begin with, but after Abbie had sat on it it looked even more ridiculous. I expect it was a bit mean of me but when I told Mum about it afterwards I giggled. I said, 'It looked like a hat that's had too much to drink!' But it serves her right for saying me and Mum live like they did in the 1940.

Anyway, that is all about the party. I hope you enjoyed it. Now I want to hear about your visit to the British Museum! And see how quickly you can get into my maze.

Loadsa luv,
Katie.

PS   Here is
another joke.
   What do sea
monsters
eat?
   Fish and
ships!

   Ho ho!

Here is my
drawing from
the Scribble.

Hi, Katie!

You sound like you had really good fun at the party! My friend Sarah had a DJ last year but I don't think it was the same one. I cannot remember his name, but he didn't look like Prince Charles! I would remember if he had.

Our visit to the British Museum was totally brilliant! We saw all these ancient old mummies wrapped up in bandages. Quite s-s-s-scary! But very interesting, of course. Now we have to write our mummy stories. Lily says she is going to write one about a mummy that starts pouring 'fountains of blood' out of his eyes. It is a mad mummy! Somehow or other it gets hold of a chain saw and starts running all about the museum sawing people in half. She says there are going to be 'arms and legs chopped off and intestines spilling out'. You might think this shows what a great imagination she has, but in fact it was in a film we once saw, so all she is really doing is just copying.

My story is going to be about a sad

mummy. He is a mummy who is suddenly brought back to life and can't understand where he is, or why he is shut up in a glass case with everybody staring at him. He misses his wife and children. He doesn't realise that he has been dead for thousands of years. I will have to work out a happy ending, though, as I wouldn't want him to suffer for all eternity.

I must tell you that it was really funny, while we were at the museum. For starters, me and Sarah got a bit hyper on the train going there. We couldn't stop giggling! We giggled at just about everything. Mrs Frost told us to behave ourselves or she would send us back to school, so that quietened us down a bit until we got to the museum and then, oh dear! We discovered a mummy that looked exactly like this really nerdy teacher that we have called Mr Spooner. He is very dry and withered, like a piece of old twig. Or like a mummy! If you wrapped him in bandages, you wouldn't be able to tell the difference. It was Sarah that saw him first. She showed him to me, and before I could stop myself I had cried, 'Mr Spooner! What is he doing here?' Everyone just collapsed into mad giggles. Even Mrs Frost nearly laughed, I saw her lips twitch! She told us that we were the very worst bunch she had ever had to deal with.

I hope she doesn't put it in my report!

We are just having half-term now. A week after everyone else I don't know why we always seem to have different holidays from other schools. I am not doing anything special. Lily has gone away with one of her posh friends to a cottage they have. They are going to ride ponies and go to gymkhanas, and be all hectic. I could have gone if I had wanted, but I decided I would rather just stay at home. I have lots of things to do. Such as:

Sticking things in my scrapbook
Sorting photographs
Helping mum in Flora Green
Writing to you!

Please don't worry about not having a computer. I would rather write real letters and don't mind if it is snail mail. I think that girl that you told me about, Carrie Francis, was extremely rude to say how did you survive.

Your maze that you sent me was HEAPS harder than the first one. I had to start it three times before I could find the way in. It was a really good one and I wish I could do one for you but I have tried and I can't. So here is another word game. Can you find which flowers these are:

Uptil   Sore   Drogmail
Foglevox   Shopytalun
I think the last one is quite difficult!

Next weekend we are going to Visit Little Nan and Popsy. (Popsy is what we call my granddad James.) It is Little Nan's birthday. She will be the big six-oh. Sixty! All the family are going to be there. All my aunties and uncles and cousins. I will tell you about it.

I have been trying to think of a joke but I can't so here are some book titles I have made up.

DOG'S DINNER by Nora Bone
HOLE IN THE BUCKET by Lee King
HOW TO GET RICH by Robin
Banks (this one is my favourite!)

Now I have to go because Mum is
calling that tea is ready. Bye for now!
xxxxxxxxx Violet

PS The Lily that Lily is named after is
not a droopy one but a big spotty
thing about 5 metres tall!

Friday morning, Lily came home from
visiting Francine. Just in time for us all
to go down to Nan and Popsy's. Mum
and Dad were both taking the day off
work. Daphne, who looks after the
shop when Mum is not there, was left
in charge of Flora Green. I worried
that without me and Mum she wouldn't
be able to manage, as weekends are
really busy, but Mum told me to just
relax and enjoy myself.

'Talk about an old head on young
shoulders,' she said.

'She just has a strongly developed sense of duty,' said Dad, as we piled into the car. 'Which is more than I can say for some people,' he added, glancing over his shoulder at Lily.

Lily was in a sulk. Francine's mum had brought her home, but Francine's mum was then driving back down to the country because tomorrow there was some big horsy show or something that Francine was taking part in and Lily was dead resentful.

'*I* could have taken part! I could have ridden Cobbie! Francie said I could. She was going to let me borrow him! I don't see why I had to come to Nan's birthday. I went last year! Why do I have to come again?'

Mum said, 'Because it's a family thing and Nan's going to be sixty and she would be very disappointed if you weren't there.'

'But all we do is play stupid games! That's all we ever do. I could have been riding Cobbie! I bet I'd have got a rosette!'

She went on and on about it. She said it was all right for me: 'She *likes* playing stupid games.'

I do like playing games, it is true, and so does Lily when she's actually there. But she'd had such a good time with Francine I could sort of sympathise with her. She'd been riding every day. She'd helped out at the stables; she'd gone to a Pony Club meet; she'd made heaps of new friends; she'd taken Cobbie over a jump that nobody else had been able to manage; she'd only come off once—'And even then I remembered to hang on to the reins!'—and now she was thinking that instead of becoming a PA when she grew up she would enter the horsy world and ride for Britain in the Olympics.

She told us all this in the car as we drove to Nan's. Nobody else got a word in edgeways! It's always the same when Lily gets obsessed. Like the time she was going to be an ice skater, and the time she was going to be a pop star. I think to be fair to her she probably *will* be something. I mean something with a great big capital S. It just depends which particular enthusiasm she's got going when it comes time to leave school.

'Francie's mum says I have a really good seat!' bawled Lily, bouncing up and down in the back of the car and making me feel sick. 'She says I can ride Cobbie whenever I want. She says I can go down there again at Easter if I like. She says I could even go h—'

Lily stopped.

'Go what?' I said.

'Oh!' Lily waved a hand. 'Just . . . you know!'

'*Go what?*' I screeched it at her. Lily cringed back against the seat. '*Go hunting?*'

'I didn't say that,' said Lily.

'You were going to!'

'I was not!'

'You were too!'

'I was *n*—'

'Lily and Violet!' Mum turned in her seat and thundered it at us. 'Stop that! Right this minute! I don't want to hear another word. Have you got that? Not another word!'

Lily and I glared at each other. We sat the rest of the way in simmering silence. A few minutes ago I'd been half wishing that I'd told Katie it was me going to stay with Francine. I would have had so much to report! The only reason I hadn't, really, was 'cos she was just staying at home with her mum and I wouldn't have wanted it to seem like I was boasting or anything. Now I was glad! Katie felt the same way I did about fox hunting. I'd always thought Lily did, too, but she obviously didn't. Because she *had* been going to say fox hunting! She was a TURNCOAT.

I think she must have felt a bit ashamed of herself 'cos she was nice as pie to me all weekend, and when we went to bed that first night she whispered, 'You know I wouldn't really go hunting.' I was glad that she wouldn't but I did think she should have said something to Francine and her mum. I'd said something to Katie! And that was *before* I knew she was on my side. She might not have been. She might have got into a huff and never written to me again. So I just, like, grunted at Lily and pulled the duvet over my head and pretended to go to sleep. I didn't want to hear any more about her and her horsy friends!

When we got home on Sunday I looked eagerly at the front door mat to see if there was a letter for me, but there wasn't. Lily said, 'Are you expecting something from the Blob? Don't tell me you're still *snail* mailing?'

'She hasn't got a computer,' I said. 'I did ask her!' I said this for Dad's benefit. 'I said we could e-mail but she said her mum's got a lot of bills to pay and they can't afford a computer just at the moment.'

Lily looked at me like she wasn't

hearing right. 'Can't afford a *computer*?'

'She hasn't got a dad,' I said.

'Why not? Where is he?'

'I don't know. She hasn't told me.'

'You mean, you haven't asked? I would ask!'

'That would be a personal question,' I said. 'You can't ask people personal questions. Her mum and dad might be divorced.'

'So what? Lots of people's mums and dads are divorced. Francie's mum and dad are divorced. She doesn't care who knows. I'd say straight out,' boasted Lily. 'Are your mum and dad divorced? That's what I'd say. It's nothing to be ashamed of. I mean, it's nothing odd. Not like not having a computer. That is just so weird! How do they live?'

'They live just the same as anybody else,' I said, crossly.

Lily looked over at Dad and made her eyes go big. I know she was expecting him to be on her side, what with him being a computer person and all, but Dad just laughed and said,

108

'You could do with a spell on a desert island, my girl!'

Hooray! That told her.

Hi Katie,

I know it's not my turn to write but I wanted to tell you about my ace weekend with my nan and granddad.

Nan had a birthday cake with SIXTY CANDLES on it. Truly! She counted them. It was a VERY BIG cake! It took her several goes to blow out all the candles. In the end we had to help her!

What made it such fun was that all the family came and we played games. All the family is: aunties and uncles (two of each); my great aunt (Nan's sister); my cousins (six in all).

Two of my cousins are boys, but they are quite nice. This is because they are still little!!! One of them is seven and the other is five. They have not yet had time to grow horrible . . . Of my four girl cousins my favourite is Stephanie as she is like us and hates fox hunting. Stephanie is twelve. You would get on with her!

The games that we played were:

Miming

20 Questions

Charades

How does it resemble me?

This last was particularly funny! How it is played is that one person has to go out of the room and all the rest think of an object. The person then comes back and goes round in a circle asking 'How does it resemble me?' and trying to guess what it is. It was SO hilarious! When my nan went out of the room the object chosen was: a flower pot. Well, she came back and started to ask questions, and when she got to my granddad and said, 'How does it resemble me?' you will never guess what he replied! Very solemnly he said, 'It has a hole in its bottom.' Nan looked quite shocked for a moment so that I felt sure she was going to tell him off for being rude, but in the end she couldn't help laughing, and so then we all did.

Charades was also fun. In case you

don't know it, this is where you divide into teams and each team chooses a word and breaks it down into syllables. You then act out each syllable and people have to work out what the word is.

I was in a team with Stephanie, Uncle Dave, my dad and my great aunt Annie. Our word was AEROBICS. (Air-o-bix.) When we did the first syllable Aunt Annie pretended to be an opera singer (singing an AIR). She dressed up in a big lacy tablecloth and put a lamp-shade on her head! She is a very dignified sort of person—she is a head teacher!!!—and it was just hilarious. I couldn't help wondering what the children at her school would think if they could see her!

It was a really great weekend. Even Lily enjoyed it, though she was moaning like crazy on the way there as she didn't want to leave her friend Francine and miss out on riding a pony called Cobbie in a gymkhana.

What sort of things do you do when you go and visit your nan?

Where does your nan live? Mine lives in St Alban's, which is not so very far away.

Tomorrow we go back to school. WOE. I don't really mind though it would be far more fun just to go on playing charades and seeing my Aunt Annie in a lampshade! Her school had already been on half-term. We were a whole week later than everyone else but we break up a week earlier. On the other hand we do LOADS of homework and we start at half-past eight every morning and don't finish until half-past four, which I think is quite a LONG DAY.

Please write soon!

Lots of love

from your friend

Violet xxx

PS This is a joke my Uncle Dave told me. How do you make a sausage roll? Push it!

PPS Did you manage to work out all the flower words?

Hi, Violet!

Sorry I haven't written for ages.
Almost ten days! I expect you will
have been wondering what has
happened and whether you have
said something to offend me,
which is what I would most
probably be wondering if you
didn't write back to me like almost
IMMEDIATELY.

I have been in bed, boo hoo! I
have had this really bad cold and
couldn't go to school, which I
absolutely hate. There are some
people that think it is fun, not
having to go to school, but I am

not one of them! It is just so boring, lying in bed, even though Mum stayed home to keep me company. I kept thinking all the time of what was going on at school without me, and wanting so much to write to you but I just felt too woozy. Like my head was full of fog. I did try starting a letter but my hand went like

all across the page so that you wouldn't have been able to read it anyway! It was, like, all sh-sh-shivery and sh-sh-shaky. Like a g-g-g-ghost.

I am not yet back at school so I am going to write you this really LONG letter. Be warned!!!

I did your flower arrangements. (Mum says it is called ANAGRAMS,

114

when you mix up the letters of a word.)

Uptil (tulip)

Sore (rose)

Drogmail (marigold)

Foglevox (foxglove)

Shopytalun (polyanthus)

Marigold and polyanthus were really difficult! Especially as polyanthus is one I hadn't heard of . . . Mum had to help me with that one! I expect you know all about flowers because of your mum.

The flowers were in your first letter, which I expect by now you will have forgotten what you wrote. I will have to remind you!

I keep all of your letters. Do you keep mine? While I was in bed I read through all of yours and I just felt so happy that we are pen pals!

Mum says that the lily that Lily is named after is probably a TIGER lily. A tiger lily would look like this:

I still like violets best!

I couldn't help laughing about your visit to the British Museum and seeing a mummy that looked like one of your teachers! I have done a strip cartoon of it. I will stick it on now.

Next week, me and Mum are doing a sponsored walk for the Cats' Protection League. We got

Bella
and
Bertie
from them
and so that
is why we
always support
them. These are
the people I have been sponsored
by:

The lady who lives upstairs, Mrs
Cathcart. (She is old but very
nice. Sometimes if I am at home
when Mum is at school I go
upstairs and watch TV with her.)
Our next door neighbours (both

sides).

The lady in the newspaper shop.

The whole of my class at school!

If I walk right round (five miles) I will make ... £52!!! I am really looking forward to it.

I am glad you enjoyed your nan's birthday party. It sounded like fun. I specially liked Auntie Annie in the lampshade!

I told Mum about your granddad saying to your nan that 'It has a hole in its bottom'. Mum thought it was very funny! Mrs Cathcart came down on Sunday afternoon for tea and we played the game of 'How does it resemble me?' but we didn't have a flower pot! Mrs Cathcart is too old and might have been upset.

You asked me what we do when we visit my nan and where she lives. She lives in Yorkshire but we don't ever visit her. She won't have anything to do with us, except just at Christmas and on my birthday she sends me a present and I write to thank her, but that is all. She doesn't want to see us or even for me to ring her up. This is because she thinks we are beneath her. She was my dad's mum, and she was very angry when he and Mum got married.

Unfortunately she is the only nan I have as Mum was brought up in a children's home and has no family. She and Dad were so happy together! There is a photo of them holding hands and looking all smoochy into each other's eyes. But my dad died when I was only three and so I never really knew him and I have never met my nan at all as she cut us off and retired to live in her dark and spooky house and never see the light of day. Dad was her only child so perhaps when he died it unhinged her mind, but Mum says she is a very proud and unforgiving woman and so I cannot really feel too sorry for her.

Mum is the one I feel sorry for. I think it is so unkind, the way she has been treated.

You are lucky to have a mum AND a dad AND a sister (even if it is not always fun) AND two nans and a granddad. I am not being jealous when I say this but I would like to at least have a nan. Mum says Mrs Cathcart is 'as good as' but Mrs Cathcart has children of her own and always goes off at Christmas to stay with them. So then I am completely nan-less! It is just Mum and me. Even Arthur has a family.

I hope this letter doesn't sound too glum and gloomy. It is not meant to. But you did ask! About my nan, I mean. I am not feeling sorry for myself, I am just telling you how it is.

The reason you have half-term at a different time from everyone else is because you go to a posh school and posh schools do everything differently from everyone else! I expect you have to be quite rich to go to your school. I don't mind if you are rich! My nan is rich. Mum says she has more money than she knows what to do with. Mrs Cathcart says, 'It is a pity she doesn't spend some of it on her granddaughter,' but Mum says, 'We can do without her charity.'

I have not yet done another maze, but here is a joke! I just made it up.

Question: What kind of robbery is the easiest?

Answer: a safe robbery!

I think that is quite good.

And now I must tell you something. I have had this totally brilliant and earth shattering idea! You know in one of your letters you said how it would be great if you could write stories and I could do pictures to go with them? Well, we could do a magazine! Like Go Girl, only we could make it funny. You could do the writing bits and I could do the drawings. Do you think this is a good idea? We could have problem pages and letters pages and short stories and poems and articles. And then when we had done it you could maybe make copies on your computer and I would do a cover for it. Say if you want to! You don't have to. I mean, like if you're too busy or anything. Or if you think it would just be a drag. But if you would like to you could send me something next time you write and I would do the pictures straight away.

I hope this letter is not so long that you have stopped reading it! I must close now as my hand is beginning to ache. I suppose that would be one good thing about having a computer. Mum says maybe next year. I will keep my fingers crossed!

Lots of luv from

Katie xxxxxxxxxx

I told Mum about Katie's dad, and about her nan being too proud and unforgiving to have anything to do with

Katie and her mum. (I didn't tell Lily as she was still calling Katie the Blob and so I didn't think she deserved to be told. Plus she would probably only say something stupid and annoying.)

'It's so sad, isn't it?' I said to Mum.

Mum agreed that it was. 'But it's nice that she's told you. She obviously felt ready for it. And it explains why she's always seemed so close to her mum, if there's only the two of them.'

'At least she has Arthur and Mrs Cathcart,' I said. 'I know it's not the same, but it's better than nothing.'

I was so excited by Katie's idea of writing stories and poems for our own magazine. It is just exactly the sort of thing that I really love to do! I sat down immediately and wrote a poem and sent it to her.

123

Dear Katie,

I will write a proper letter soon. I
love the idea of doing a magazine!
Here is a poem I have written for it.
  xxx Violet

PS   What shall we call it? The
Magazine, I mean.

POEM

I'M HAVING A VERY BAD HAIR
    DAY,
MY HAIR SIMPLY LOOKS A SIGHT!
IT STICKS UP IN SPOKES, ALL
    OVER THE PLACE,
IT WON'T DO ANYTHING
    RIGHT!

OH, WHAT CAN I DO WITH MY
    HORRIBLE HAIR,
HOW CAN I MAKE IT BEHAVE?
I'M OFF TO A PARTY
    TOMORROW,
IT'S GOING TO BE QUITE A
    GOOD RAVE!

HOW CAN I GO WITH MY HAIR
    IN THIS STATE?
IT IS SUCH A TERRIBLE MESS!
AND TO THINK I'VE BOUGHT
    SOME NEW SHOES,
AND A HUGELY EXPENSIVE NEW
    DRESS!

I KNOW WHAT I'LL DO! I'VE
    GOT A GOOD PLAN.
I WON'T GO AND SULK IN MY
    BED.
I'LL INVENT A NEW FASHION,
    I'LL BE REALLY COOL,
I'LL JUST WEAR A CAT ON MY
    HEAD!

Dear Violet,

Your poem is really funny! It made
me laugh. I have tried to draw
some funny pictures for it. I hope
you like them.

xxx Katie

PS   How about GIRLZONE
(Girls' Own . . . Girlzone! Geddit?)
But you can suggest something
else if you prefer.

Hi, Katie!

The pictures are ace! And I think
GIRLZONE is cool. Now I have
made up some problems for a
problem page. I will type them out
on the computer and send them
with this letter. But I have not done
the answers as I think it would be
better if you did those.

Your last letter that you wrote me
was not in the least glum and gloomy
though I am sorry if I upset you by
asking about your nan. I know that I
am very lucky to have a family even if
I do sometimes complain about my
sister. She is quite a tiresome sort of
person, but in future I will try to
complain a bit less and just put up
with her.

It is true you have to pay to go to
my school, but we are not rich!!!
Mum said to Lily just the other day
that 'We are not made of money'.
This was because Lily was nagging
about these new riding boots she
wants. She says her old ones are naff,
and she can't be seen in them. She

127

has to have SPECIAL ones like her friend Francine has. So Mum told her she couldn't and Lily got into one of her sulks and that was when Mum snapped we weren't made of money.

I have asked Mum if we can sponsor you for your walk! She says that we can and we would like to give you a pound for every mile. Just let me know how many you do! We got Horatio from a lady that comes into Mum's shop, but if ever we get another cat we will go to the Cats' Protection League. That is a promise!

I look forward to hearing your answers to my problems!

Luv and kisses (lots of them)
from
Violet

PS   I keep all your letters, too! In a special box with a LOCK.

PROBLEM PAGE

Dear Katie,
My sister has such a big head that if I walk behind her no one can see me. What do you think I should do? Please help!—*Norah Nobody.*

Dear Katie,
I have a confession to make . . . I am frightened of my own shadow. This is so pathetic! How can I cure myself?—*Scaredy Cat.*

Dear Katie,
When I go to parties I stand in the corner and nobody talks to me. How can I make myself more noticeable?—*Mouse.*

Ever since the incident with the riding boots, Mum and Lily had been on *really* bad terms. Lily, as usual, said that Mum was ruining her life, because how could she hope to be a top class rider and ride for Britain if she didn't have the proper riding boots. Mum said the riding boots she had were perfectly adequate and that Lily was a spoilt brat.

She said, 'Sometimes I wonder why your dad and I bother! We work our fingers to the bone, all the hours God sends, and what for? Just so that you can go to your snotty little school and mix with your snotty little friends and be thoroughly grasping and disagreeable!'

Wow!

She said she had a good mind to take Lily away from Lavendar House and send her to the local comprehensive.

'Why just me?' said Lily. 'What about little Shrinky Winky? Of course, *she* couldn't go to the comprehensive, could she? She's too *delicate.* She'd get *crushed.*'

'I could go there!' I said. Though as a matter of fact I am the reason that Mum and Dad work their fingers to the bone and send us to our snotty little school. (Which is quite nice, really.) It is because of me being a shrinking violet and Mum being scared that I couldn't cope. Which maybe I couldn't.

The thought of being with *boys*, and lots of tough kids, is scary. It wouldn't scare Lily. She'd be all right! She'd be one of the tough kids.

But she was really resentful.

'Why just *me*? Why is it always *me*?'

'Because Violet doesn't constantly make demands,' said Mum.

'No, 'cos she never does anything!' screeched Lily. 'She just sits upstairs writing letters to the Blob!'

'I'm not just writing letters,' I said. 'We're doing a magazine. We're going to call it GIRLZONE . . . Girls' Own. Geddit?'

Lily said, 'Hey! That's quite cool,' in tones of some surprise. She then got a bit sidetracked, wanting to know when the magazine was going to be finished and what sort of things were going to be in it and whether we were going to have any articles about horses.

' 'Cos if you like, I could do one for you.'

I said that I would ask Katie, though to be honest I didn't really think we wanted anything about horses, I mean it wasn't a *horsy* mag, and I definitely didn't think I wanted Lily interfering.

'Well, just let me know,' said Lily. 'I could do you a really good article about riding boots.'

She looked at Mum quite boldly as she said this. Mum snapped, 'I don't wish to hear another word! If you want to go down to Francine's again at Easter, my girl, you had just better watch your step!'

So after that, Lily started being all polite. Unnaturally polite. Like everything was *please* and *thank you* and could I *possibly*. And always with this big bright beam to show how charming she was being. Sickening, really.

One day she came home from school and said that Debbie's dad was going to take Debbie into town on Saturday and they were going to go on the London Eye and Debbie had asked Lily if she'd like to go with them.

'Of course I said I'd have to ask my mum,' gushed Lily, beaming away as hard as she could.

'You can go on the Eye,' said Mum. 'I have no objections to that.'

'Oh, how darling!' cried Lily.

Mum gave her this long look, then slowly shook her head.

'*She* could come, if she wanted,' said Lily. 'I don't s'ppose Debbie would mind.'

'Violet? Would you like to?' said Mum.

I would have done, quite. But I just knew that Lily was only saying it to get in Mum's good books. She didn't really want me.

'Just say,' said Lily. 'You've only got to say.'

' 'S all right,' I said. 'I've got things to do.'

'Violet? Are you sure?' said Mum.

'I've got to write a short story,' I said.

'Oh! Well.' Lily tossed her head. 'If you'd rather write a *short* story—'

'I've got to,' I said. 'I promised

133

Katie.'

I went upstairs to my bedroom, thinking that I would do it straight away, but I couldn't even get started! I kept thinking how I could have written a story about someone going on the London Eye, and wishing that I'd said I'd go. It would have been something to tell Katie! I am so *stupid* at times. I really annoy myself.

Dear Violet,

I have answered all your problems! I have done some pictures to go with them.

I thought that we could also, maybe, have some funny articles. But only if you feel like doing them. If you are not too busy with all your homework! I told Mum about your homework. She said, 'And a good thing too!' She really approves of your school! Ours doesn't really have homework too much, but I do lots of things with Mum, such as working out problems and reading books together. We do that quite often.

Hey, guess what? I have been invited to THREE PARTIES! Two are people in my class and one is a girl that lives over the road. I am really excited and wondering what to wear. Mum says we will go into town at the weekend and buy something. She has promised that I will get to choose! I said, 'Can I choose whatever I like?' She said, 'Anything so long as it is decent.' That means anything! 'cos I wouldn't want not to be decent, would you?

What I would really really REALLY like is this fab top I saw someone wearing, white with gold fringes, and these really swanky jeans with a sparkly belt. Oh, and come zip-up trainers! Pink ones. That is what I would REALLY like. I will tell you if I get them!!!

Must dash.

Oodles of love!

xxx Katie

PTO FOR PROBLEM PAGE.

[ANSWERS]

Dear Norah,
Do not despair! The solution is simple. FIND YOURSELF A PIN. A quick sharp JAB will soon deflate your sister's head.
Good luck!

Dear Scaredy Cat,
There are several things you can try. First off you could avoid going out on days when there is sunshine, then there would not be any shadow for you to be scared of. However, this may not always be convenient. How about suddenly spinning round and shouting 'Boo!' very loudly and fiercely? That would see it off!

Alternatively you could try saying 'Hi!' It might turn out to be friendly. You never know!

Dear Mouse,
Learn some kind of social skill. For instance you could:

Walk on your hands. But do make sure you are wearing clean knickers without any holes!

Juggle with plates. Though maybe oranges would be safer, just to begin with.

Belch in time to God Save the Queen. This would soon get people's attention!

Try any of these and before you know it everyone will be desperate to talk to you!

Dear Katie,

I thought your answers to my problems were really funny! I love the idea of belching in time to God Save the Queen. I have tried doing it but I can't belch! Lily can. She does it all the time and says it is quite easy. She has tried to teach me but all I do is gulp down air and make myself ill. Lily says I am useless. She says I have no social skills at all.

When are your, parties that you are going to? I don't know whether Lily and me will have a party this year. Last year when we had one Lily got hyper and threw Ribena all over the wall and trod on a glass and smashed the banisters. How she smashed the banisters, she was pretending to ride a horse. She was going 'Giddyap, giddyap,' and kicking at the banister rails. Mum and Dad were just so furious with her! Mum said she was a vandal and Dad said she ought to live in a hole at the bottom of the garden. So I don't know whether we will have one this year. But I want to hear all about your ones!

My news is that I am going to go on the London Eye. I think this will be quite exciting! I am going with a friend from school called Debbie. Her dad is taking us. I just hope I don't get sick, which is what I usually do. Like one time when Dad took us on a Giant Octopus where you sat in this little pod thing at the end of a long arm, and the arm went up in the air like a big wheel and at the same time the little pod thing whizzed round and round incredibly fast. It made me feel sick as sick! I

just couldn't wait to get off. And
then when I did, you'll never guess
what . . . I instantly threw up all over
Lily! Boy, was she ever mad! But the
Eye moves really s . . . l . . . o . . . w . . .
l . . . y, so that you hardly even
notice, so maybe I will be all right. I
would not like to throw up over
Debbie's dad!

Here is a pattern I have done for
Girlzone.

How to sew yourself a groovy
cushion cover:

What you will need:
One of your dad's shirts (if he will
let you have one. If not, see if he has
put one out for rags. Do not use one
of his best ones!!!)
Needle and thread
Stuff for filling

What to do:
1. Lay the shirt flat.
2. Chop off the top bit, from
underneath the arms. Chuck this bit
away.

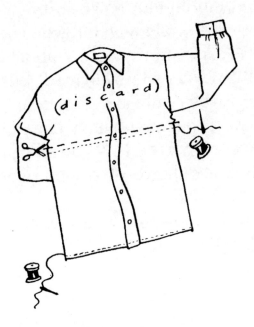

3. Take the bit that's left and turn it inside out.
4. Sew the two sides together.
5. Open the buttons and turn it back the right war.
6. Stuff with rags or cotton wool. 7. Hide a dog's sqeaky toy inside and do up the buttons.

You now have a groovy cushion that will make a loud squeeeeek! when anyone sits on it. Fun for parties! I have not tried this out as I am not very good at sewing, but I think it would be quite easy.

Anyway, we can use it if you want. We don't have to.

Please tell me about your parties. Did you get your top that you wanted? And your jeans and the trainers?

Luv from Violet xxxxxxxxxx

PS   Next I am going to do a short story!

Hiya, Violet! Groovy cushion cover!

Here is Lily riding the banisters.
Will write soon.

xxx Katie

Dear Katie,

Here is a short story. Hope you like it.
Luv Violet

PS What happened about your sponsored walk? How many miles did you do? Tell me and we will send you the money!

BETSY BURP,
by Violet Alexander

A story in 4 parts

Part 1
Once upon a time there were two sisters. One of them was called Nasturtium, the other was called Geranium. Nasturtium was known as Nasty, while Geranium was known as Gerry.

Nasty was quite nasty. She could often be really mean to her sister.

Gerry was quite merry! At least, she was when Nasty wasn't being

142

nasty to her.

One day when the girls came home from school their mother said, 'Guess what? I have just seen a notice in the *Radio Times* about a singing contest. It is going to be on television, in front of millions of viewers! The viewers will vote who is the winner, and they will be given a contract with a big record company and become famous overnight. Gerry, you have a nice loud voice! Why don't you enter the contest?'

'I will!' cried Gerry. 'What a cool idea! I will sing my favourite song and perhaps I will win and become famous!'

Nasty sniffed and said, 'Dream on!'

She was just jealous because her mum had not said that she had a nice loud voice. Nasty did have a loud voice, as a matter of fact, but it wasn't very nice. Whenever she started to sing people would stuff their fingers in their ears and go 'Ow!' and 'Ouch!' and 'This is so painful!'

But Nasty was of the opinion she had a perfectly wonderful voice. Far better than her sister's.

'I will go in for the contest as well,' she thought. 'But I will not tell her.'

Part 2

The day of the singing contest arrived. Gerry was so nervous she didn't want to eat anything, but her mum said she must or she would feel faint.

'Nasty,' she said, 'go and make your sister a sandwich.'

'Oh, if I must,' said Nasty.

Nasty made the sandwich out of hard-boiled eggs, all mashed up with salt and pepper, oil of cloves, mustard, soya sauce, tomato ketchup, and . . . garlic! Six whole cloves of it. Yeeeeurgh!

'Tee hee!' thought Nasty. 'This sandwich will make her puke, for sure!'

But Gerry was in such a state she didn't even notice.

'Is it all right?' said Nasty.

'Yes. Thank you. It is very yummy,' said Gerry, wondering why Nasty was suddenly being so nice to her.

After she had eaten the sandwich,

Gerry and her mum left for the TV studio. On the way there Gerry came over a bit peculiar, but she thought that it was just nerves.

'Once I start to sing,' she thought, 'I will feel better.'

She was going to sing her favourite song, Love ya, baby! These were the words:

Love ya, baby!
I sure do.
Don't want her.
Just want you!
Trust me, babe!
It's me 'n you.

She had sat up all night learning them.

When they reached the studio there were dozens of really cool kids there, all hoping to become famous. They took one look at Gerry (who by now had turned quite green thanks to the mustard, oil of cloves, soya sauce, tomato ketchup and garlic sandwich) and curled their lips.

'Look at her!' they went. 'What

145

chance does she think she stands?'

'None!' came a voice from the doorway.

Gerry turned, with a gasp. It was Nasty! What was she doing there?

Part 3

'Ha, ha,' sneered Nasty. 'You didn't expect me, did you?'

Gerry shook her head. She was beginning to feel very odd and weird.

'The minute you left I jumped into a cab and followed you,' said Nasty. 'My voice is far louder than yours! I will be the pop star, not you!'

Gerry opened her mouth to say something, but all that came out was a big . . . BURP! Ugh, phew! The smell of garlic was so strong that Gerry's poor mum instantly passed out with the stench.

'Tee hee!' giggled Nasty. 'That will teach her a lesson!'

Nasty could not forgive her mum for putting Gerry in for the contest instead of her.

Gerry turned to her sister. She opened her mouth—and another burp came out. Yeeeeeeurgh!!! It was even stinkier than the first one. Nasty promptly joined her mum on the floor. She was out for the count!

And now all the other contestants were plopping down. All those really cool kids that had curled their lips! They were dropping like flies. The smell was too much!

Very soon, Gerry was the only one left . . .

Part 4

Gerry felt a whole lot better, now that she was getting rid of some of the garlic fumes. But she still couldn't stop burping! How could she sing Love ya, baby! if she was burping all the time?

The answer was—she couldn't! She had to think quickly. There were millions of viewers out there, waiting to be entertained. And all the other contestants were flat on the floor. It was up to Gerry!

So guess what she did? She burped her way through three whole verses of God Save the Queen! (She only knew the words to the first verse, but it didn't really matter as she wasn't singing them.)

Burp burp burp BURP burp burp
Burp burp burp BURP burp burp
Burp burp burp burp.

Nobody had ever heard anything like it! The clapometers went mad! And of course Gerry won the contest, because who else was there?

Now she is famous. She has changed her name to Betsy Burp, and even has her own backing group . . . Betsy Burp and the Belchers!

THE END

Dear Katie,

I hope you liked my short story that I sent you last week. Maybe you have not had time to read it yet. I expect you are very busy going to parties.

I have been on the London Eye! I was not sick as it really does go slowly so that you hardly know you are moving. The view is amazing, you can see all over London.

Well, that is all for now. Please write back soon!

xxx Violet

PS You never said how many miles you walked but here is a cheque for the cats.

Dear Violet,

I am sorry I have not written sooner. I read 'Betsy Burp' at once and it is brilliant! I nearly died laughing, and so did Mum. We think you are so clever to be able to write like that. I will do some drawings as soon as I can but I may not be able to do them for a little while. But I will do them! This is a PROMISE.

My big big huge GINORMOUS news is that I may be coming to your school in September!!! My gran has said that she will pay for me! You will probably wonder how this can have happened when I told you that my gran is proud and unforgiving and will have nothing to do with us. Well, she has changed her mind! It is so amazing! This is how it happened.

Mum picked up the phone and there she was, at the other end of it. Shock horror and wonders will never cease!!! She asked Mum if she could speak to ME. I was quite nervous, to tell you the truth. I am not usually a nervous sort of person, but I couldn't think what I would say to her. I felt that I hated her because of the way she has treated Mum, but at the same time she is my gran and I have always wanted to have a gran. So I picked up the receiver and said 'Hallo'?' in what I hoped was a NONDESCRIPT way, like not cross, exactly, but not friendly, either, in case she was going to say something mean about Mum, but she didn't. You'll never guess what she did . . . she APOLOGISED!!!

She said that she was really sorry about not speaking to us all these years. She said, 'I'm just a stupid stiff-necked old woman and you must try to forgive me.' So I did, which I hope you won't think was weak of me but she is my gran and she did say sorry. To me AND to Mum. I think this may be because she is growing old and is feeling all alone in the world. She says that now we have 'broken the ice' we must behave like a real family before it is too late and so she is going to come and visit with us, and then later on we are going to go and visit with her. I will tell you all about it!

After she had finished speaking to me she spoke to Mum. They were on the phone for simply ages. I heard Mum telling her all about your school and how lovely it is, and my gran said it sounded just the place for me. She said that she would get in touch immediately, and she did. The very same day! They said they have some girls that are leaving at the end of this term and they think that they will be able to take me!

I am so excited! It will be such fun! I do hope we will be in the same class, then we can sit together and do things together and be best friends. If you would like to, that is. Mum says you probably already have best friends and I mustn't push myself in, so please say if you have and I will understand. We can just go on being pen pals if you would rather. It will still be fun. I can't wait for September!!!

Lots and loads of love
from your pen pal, Katie

PS   Thank you very much for the cheque for the cats. Please say thank you to your mum.

PPS Mum is typing this letter for me on her typewriter. I am dictating it to her! This is so it can be done quickly. Also it will be easier to read!

I was thrown into deadly panic when I got Katie's letter. I know I should have been happy for her about her gran, but all I could think of was *me*. My stomach went blurp! and my heart went *thunk*. I was filled with a bottomless pit of total despair. I knew that if I told Mum—'Katie's coming to my school!'—she would say, 'Oh, isn't that lovely?' But it wouldn't be lovely! It would be a disaster! She would discover how dim and nerdy I was and how it was Lily and not me that went to parties and had been on the Eye and had best friends. She would utterly despise me and never want to talk to me again. She might even team up with Lily! I didn't think I could bear it if she did that.

I had to write to her *immediately*.

Dear Katie,

I am really happy that you liked my story. I will look forward to seeing the pictures but I quite understand if you are too busy at the moment.
   I was surprised to hear about your

gran paying for you to come to my school! I don't think you would like my school very much. For a start (I may have told you this before) it is absolutely TITCHY. We don't even have our own playing field, and for swimming we have to go to the local baths. Also there is no sixth form. I think maybe your gran does not realise this and if she did she would not want to send you there.

Mum said about it the other day that it was 'a snotty little school'. I think if you are used to going to a real school you would find it rather piddling. It is not really posh. I mean it is not where members of the Royal Family would go. It is just three ancient houses knocked together, and the teachers are quite ancient also. Like some of them have been here since practically Victorian times, I would think. They are not in the least bit cool!

Another thing is that there are of course no boys, which is quite nice at the moment as I am not into boys but I cannot help feeling that later on, when you are say twelve or thirteen, you might wish that there were otherwise how will you ever get to know about them?

I do not want to put you off or anything but your gran might not know what it is like and then she would feel that she had wasted her money and you would be disappointed and wish you had gone to a proper school. I thought I should tell you. It is only fair. We can still go on being pen pals!

Please write as soon as you are not too busy.

With luv and xxx
Violet

PS   Have you been to any of your parties yet?

Every day when I came home from school I looked for letters on the mat, but all there ever was was stuff for Mum and Dad. Nothing at all for me. One day there was even a letter for *Lily*.

'Mine!' She snatched it from me.

'Stinking swizzlesticks! Snail mail!'

All it was was a form for her to fill in if she wanted to take part in some boring gymkhana. Not a real letter at all. I'd hoped so much that it might be for me.

'Hey! What's happened to the Blob?' said Lily. 'Why don't you ever hear from her any more?'

There are times when me and Lily can almost seem to read each other's minds. I suppose it's what comes from being part of the same egg, even though we are now completely different.

'You haven't had any snaily mail in ages,' said Lily. 'You used to practically write whole *books*.' Lily folded up her letter and carefully slotted it back in its envelope. I watched her, jealously. 'I suppose you've got bored. You wouldn't get bored if you e-mailed.'

'I told you,' I said. 'She hasn't got a computer.'

'Oh!' Lily clapped a hand to her mouth. 'Sorry! I was forgetting.'

And then she gave this silly snigger and said, 'You could always try smoke signals!'

'Lily, leave Violet alone,' said Mum.

'I'm not *touching* her,' said Lily. 'I'm just trying to be helpful, is all.'

Huh! Like she would know how.

Dear Katie,

It seems ages since I heard from you. I hope I didn't upset you by saying about my school and how I didn't think you'd like it. I didn't mean to!

Here is a joke:

What do birds eat for their breakfast?
Tweet-a-bix and shredded tweet!

Hope to hear from you soon
xxx Violet

'Still no letter from Katie?' said Mum.

I made a mumbling sound.

'Why don't you try ringing her?'

'Don't know her number,' I said.

'You could look her up in the telephone directory. Why don't you give it a go? Go and get the book,' said Mum, 'and we'll look her up!'

'I don't want to,' I said.

'Why not? You haven't quarrelled, have you?'

I shook my head.

'Well, go on, then! Go and get the phone book.'

'*I DON'T WANT TO!*'

I yelled it at Mum and rushed from the room. I'm not like Lily, I don't very often yell at Mum, but I hate it when she tries to force me to do things. Like when she tries to force me into going places with Lily, when I just know that Lily doesn't want me to. I really hate it when she does that.

All the same, it did worry me that I hadn't heard from Katie for so long. I was really scared that I had upset her.

Friday was the end of term and we were let out early. Lily went off with Francine, so I thought I would have to go to Flora Green by myself to pick up Mum, but instead I found that she was waiting for me outside school. I was quite surprised.

'Mum!' I said. 'What are you doing?'

'Jump in,' said Mum. 'I left work early. Listen, I had a telephone call today . . . at the shop. It was Katie's mum.'

'K-Katie's m-*mum*?' I said; and my blood went all to water and my knees went wobbly. Why would Katie's *mum* be ringing?

'The reason you haven't heard from Katie,' said Mum, 'is that she's been in hospital. Don't look so alarmed! She's had to have an operation, but she's going to be all right.'

I swallowed. 'What s-sort of operation?'

'Well, it seems she's had a weak heart for a very long time—'

'*Katie?*'

I couldn't believe it! In her letters she had always sounded so full of life and energy. I had really admired her for it. I had envied her! How could *Katie* have a weak heart?

Mum explained that it was something she'd been born with and that it had just been getting worse and worse until in the end an operation had been necessary.

'But she's come through it and she's going to be fine. Her mum says she's fretting because she hasn't been able to write to you. She says having you as a pen pal has made all the difference to her these last few months, when she's been so ill. Now she's worried in case you think she doesn't want to be her friend any more. So what we've arranged—'

'W—what?' I said.

'We're going to go over there tomorrow, so that you can pay her a visit. OK?'

'No!' I didn't want to! I didn't want to!

'Violet, she's your friend!' said Mum. 'And she's in hospital. It's what you do when your friends are in hospital . . . you go and visit them. Try to cheer them up.'

'I could send her a card,' I said. 'A funny one!'

'She doesn't want a funny card, she wants a visit. She wants to *see* you. So we're going over there,' said Mum. 'Tomorrow afternoon.'

'But what about the shop?' I wailed.

'Don't worry about the shop,' said Mum. 'The shop can take care of itself.'

'But it's busy on a Saturday!'

'Violet,' said Mum. She pulled the car up at some traffic lights. 'Katie is your *friend*. You owe her this! Oh! And something you didn't tell me,' she said, as the lights changed, 'I gather she's going to Lavendar House in September. That will be fun! Won't it? The two of you together. That will really be something to look forward to!'

All that night I stayed awake, worrying. Worrying is a thing that I do quite often. I don't think Lily has ever worried about anything in the whole of her life. I wish I could be more like her!

No, I don't; not really. I just wish I could be a little bit less like me!

Well, sometimes I do.

You'll never believe it, but when we set out next day Lily actually clamoured to come with us.

'I want to see the Blob! I could cheer her up. *She* won't cheer her up! She'll just make her miserable. Oh, Mum, please! Let me come to the hospital with you!'

But Mum wouldn't let her. Thank goodness!

'Katie is Violet's friend,' she said, 'not yours.'

I couldn't help wondering whether she would still want to be, once she'd discovered the truth . . .

Saturday

Dear Violet,

I was so ☺ to see you today! It was quite a surprise—Mum didn't tell me you were coming so I was truly amazed when the door

opened and you walked in. You
were just how I imagined you
from your letters! I wonder if I was
how you imagined me? I don't
expect I was, but I hope I didn't
come as a huge disappointment. I
really really REALLY loved
meeting you! I felt very ☹ when
you had to go. Please come again
soon!

I was deathly ashamed when
your mum said about me doing
that sponsored walk for the cats
and Mum said, 'Oh, it was so sad,
she was too ill to do it.' I felt so
dreadful! Like a thief, or a cheat. I
should have told you. I don't know
why I didn't! I meant to, but then
you sent the money and I was just
so pleased that I gave it to Mum
for the cats and I didn't tell her
that I hadn't told you and now she
says it was very wrong of me as it
was getting money under false
pretences and I must ask you if
you would like it back. She says
we will send you a cheque AT
ONCE. She also says that I must

apologise to your mum, so please will you say to her that I apologise? I see now that it was a very bad thing to do. I just so much wanted to help the poor cats!

Next week I am going to be back home and I will draw some pictures for 'Betsy Burp' which I LOVE! I will send them to you as soon as I have done them.

Please say if you would like the cat money back and say sorry for me to your mum.

Love and lots of xxxxxx
From Katie

Saturday (same day as Katie wrote to me!)

Dear Katie,

We have just got back after seeing you. I was really shocked when Mum told me yesterday about you being ill and having to have an operation. I have never known anyone before that has had to have one. I think it

164

must be very scary. I would be scared!

But I expect you are a lot braver than me. Like Lily. She is brave. She would not be scared by anything! If you had told me I would have sent you a card. I would have sent LOTS of cards. One a day! With messages and jokes to cheer you up. But I can understand why you didn't. It was probably something you didn't want to think about. If I was going to have an operation I would do my best to pretend it wasn't happening. I am glad it is all over and that you are now better.

I was quite scared of meeting you. I am afraid I am a bit of a scaredy cat about all kinds of things. What I was scared of was that I would not be able to think of anything to say, which is this thing that happens when I meet people for the first time, and especially if they have had an operation and might still be feeling poorly so you are not sure how to behave. I hope I did not seem too stupid.

165

You know when our mums were talking and your mum was saying about how you couldn't do things and it was so frustrating for you, and my mum said how I COULD do things but I wouldn't, such as for example going into town with Lily and her friend Debbie and going on the London Eye? I could tell that you were really surprised when she said this. I could tell that your mum was surprised, too. I am sorry I told you that I went on the Eye when it was Lily that did. I expect now you will think I am totally mad.

Mum says why doesn't she take you and me on the Eye some time? She says to ask if you would like to do this. (As soon as you are well enough.) I would like it, but I will understand if you would rather not. I am really sorry that I told you a lie.

I hope you will still want to write to me. I promise I will not tell you any more lies about things that I have done that I have not really done.

With love from
Violet

Hi, Violet,

I just got your letter. Did you get mine? Mum says they must have 'crossed in the post'.

I was not scared of having an operation as they put you to sleep and so you know nothing about it. I am more scared when I go to the dentist and they stick needles in you. I hate it when they stick needles in you! I go AAAh and OOOh and OUCH! Mum says I am a real baby.

I am sorry if I did not tell you. Mum says I should have done (as you are my friend) but if I had said at the beginning that I could not do things I thought maybe you would say to yourself this girl is no fun, I do not want to write to her. So that is why I didn't tell you. But I am very sorry.

I suppose I was a LITTLE bit surprised when your mum said about it being Lily that went on the Eye and not you, but it really doesn't matter. I don't think you are mad. But if you are, then I am too, 'cos I told you that I went to Susanna's party and danced and did the limbo contest and played games, and I didn't. I went to the party but mostly all I did was just sit and watch. Next time I go I will be able to join in! But it wasn't quite the truth, what I told you, so I am glad you pretended you had gone on the Eye as now that makes us equal!

I would love to go with you and your mum! Mum says not this week but maybe next, if that would be convenient for you.

Now there is something I have to ask you. It is about your school. I know you said you weren't trying to put me off but then Mum said about you probably already having best friends, like Sarah that you mentioned, and I thought maybe you might not want me coming there. I am sorry, it is too late for me to go anywhere else as my gran has already fixed it all up, but I just wanted to say that I will not try to come between you and Sarah. We do not have to sit together or do things together if you would rather not. I hope this makes it all right.

Write soon!

xxx Katie

PS   Here are the pictures I have done for 'Betsy Burp and the Belchers'.

Dear Katie,

Thank you for your letter saying that you were ☺ to see me. I was ☺ to see you! I am glad Mum made me go. I didn't want to at first because of being such a scaredy cat but I am going to try and be braver in future.

This morning I got your second letter that you wrote! Mum says next week would be fine for going on the Eye. If you still want to come, that is.

The reason for me saying if you still want to come is because you may not want to when I have told you something. This is what I have to tell you. Sarah that I talked about is not my friend, she is Lily's. Lily has loads of friends. It is Lily who races about going to parties. I am more like the girl in our problem page. I expect when you come to our school it will be Lily you will want to be friends with, not me. I am not being self-pitying, but I thought I should tell you. I would not like you to come to our school and think that you have

to be my friend if you don't want to.
That is all.

It was very silly of me to tell you
lies. It is not the same as you saying
you played games at the party. It
must have been so sad for you when
you couldn't, but I am just stupid.

I am very sorry I have said that I
have done things when I haven't.
Pleage tell me if you would like to
come on the Eye. Lily says it is fun.
But I will understand if you don't.
xxx Violet

PS   You can come on the Eye
without having to be my friend at
school. You can still be friends with
Lily.

'Did you ask Katie?' said Mum, next
morning.

'About what?' I said.

'About coming on the Eye,' said
Mum.

'Yes, I asked her,' I said.

'And what did she say?'

'She said . . .' I crossed my fingers
behind my back. 'She'll let me know.

She's got to ask her mum.'

'Maybe I'll give her mum a ring.'

'No!' I screeched it. Mum looked at me in surprise.

'Why not? We ought to get it organised. I'll have to arrange things at the shop.'

'But she hasn't *said*. We have to wait till she *says*.'

'Why? Why can't I just ask her mum?'

'Because she might not want to!'

I yelled it at the top of my voice and rushed from the room. Mum was doing it again! Trying to push me. She didn't know that I'd told all those stupid lies. She didn't know that I'd been found out and that most probably Katie wouldn't ever want to speak to me again. *I* wouldn't want to speak to me again. Not if I'd been lied to.

I'd just reached the top of the stairs when I heard the telephone start to ring.

I'd just reached my bedroom when

Mum called to me.

'Violet! It's for you.'

'M-me?' I peered over the banisters.

'It's Katie.'

Katie! Ringing to say she didn't want to come on the Eye. That she didn't ever want to speak to me again.

'Well, hurry up!' said Mum. 'Don't keep her waiting.'

Reluctantly, I trailed back down the stairs. Mum handed me the receiver.

'It's all right,' she said. 'I won't listen!'

I waited till Mum had left the room.

'H-hallo?' I said.

'Violet?' said Katie.

'Y-yes.'

'This is Katie.'

'K-Katie,' I said.

'Hi!'

'H-hi.'

There was a pause; then Katie giggled.

'I thought you said you were going to

173

try and be braver!'

I curled my toes. 'I am!'

'Sounds like it,' she said. 'This is only *me*. Not a man-eating tiger! Did you like my pictures for Betsy Burp? You didn't say! Does that mean you didn't like them?'

'No,' I said. 'I loved them!'

'Well, I hope you did 'cos I've done some more! And why are you trying to stop me coming on the Eye?'

I said, 'I'm not trying to s-stop you!'

'Just as well,' said Katie, ' 'cos I'm coming! My mum's going to ring yours and we're going to arrange a day. And stop trying to push me off on Lily! I don't want to be friends with Lily. All her friends are posh. That's what you said.'

'Yes,' I said. 'They are.'

'Well, I'm not,' said Katie, 'so I don't s'ppose she'd want to be friends with me anyway. And listen! I've got some more ideas for Girlzone. I thought we could have interviews with celebs. First I could be one, then you could be one, and we could ask each other questions. Like what is your star sign and what

174

is your favourite TV programme and stuff like that. Who would you want to be? I'm going to be a pop star. Listen! This is me singing . . .'

A horrible slurpy sound came oozing down the telephone at me.

'What do you think?'

I couldn't tell if she was being serious, or not.

'Think it'll make the Top Ten?'

I decided to be brave, and take a chance.

'Not drooling like that!' I said.

'New kind of music . . . drooly music. I'll be a drooler!'

'You'll be Adrooler?'

'Adroola the Drooler!'

I giggled.

'You'll have to write me some drooly songs to sing.'

'They won't just be drooly,' I said, 'they'll be truly drooly!'

Lily had just come into the room. She gave me this irritated look.

'What's going on?'

She wasn't used to me having private conversations on the telephone. She was the one that was supposed to do all the talking!

'Who is it?' she hissed. 'Is it the Blob?'

'No,' I said. 'It's Adroola.'

'Who's Adroola?'

'Adroola the Drooler. She's a pop star. Listen!'

I held out the receiver. Katie's voice came drooling down the line. Rather disgusting, actually. It sounded like someone belching into a bowl of syrup.

'Have you gone mad?' said Lily.

I shouted, 'Yes! Raving!' and danced about in front of her with my eyes crossed and one hand held up like a claw. Lily stared at me, with her mouth gaping open.

'Raving! Raving! *Bluurgh!*'

'Mum! She's gone completely mad!' wailed Lily.

'Has she?' said Mum. 'Well, I shouldn't worry about it. She seems quite happy.'

'But people might think I'm mad!' said Lily. 'They might think she's me!'

*   *   *

It is true that just lately people do seem to have started getting us more muddled up than they used to. Even, sometimes, people at school. I can't think why, since we are not in the least bit alike. Lily will tell you that I am completely mad. It is since knowing Katie. She gets you that way! She is so bright and bubbly, she makes me bright and bubbly, too.

It is such fun to have a friend! We do all kinds of things together. I've slept over at Katie's place, she's slept over at mine. (Lily was excluded. But I might let her in on it next time. If she behaves herself!)

What else have we done? We've been shopping together. Lots of times! We really enjoy shopping. We've been on the Eye. At last—and for real! Not just in my imagination. We've been ice skating! (Katie's mum took us.) Oh, and we've written loads more for

Girlzone. We did the celebs, and we did a quiz, and we did a special interview with Adroola. Our latest thing, the thing we're working on at the moment, is Makeover of the Month. We're going to have Befores and Afters. Like this:

These are true photographs! We did all the make-up and stuff in my room, with the door barricaded so that Lily couldn't get in. She was practically foaming at the mouth! She knew something was going on, she just didn't know what. Hah! That makes a change. But I don't see why I should let her in on all my secrets.

I have lots of secrets, these days. I share them with Katie. Natch! Most of them are private giggle material, just between her and me. We go round the playground, arm in arm, giggling away together. Sometimes we giggle so much we give ourselves a stitch. People look at us as if we have taken leave of our senses. But do we care?

NO WAY!